"In this debut novel, a lonely little boy travels through strange lands in an odyssey of self discovery. . . .

There is a great deal of imaginative storytelling on display here, and kids will undoubtedly enjoy Jack's eventful journey . . . this is fundamentally and unapologetically a self-help book whose child-centric plot exists solely as the framework for heartfelt lessons about self-realization and self-acceptance that should resonate with older, stressed out readers despite the juvenile setting. . . .

An inventive children's fantasy whose earnest messages about cultivating emotional health through mindfulness target adults."—*Kirkus Reviews*

Jacob

Wishing You

Peace & Love Always

Happy Jack

By

Jacqueline J. Edgington

Happy Jack
Edgington, Jacqueline. J.
Author/Publisher
Florida, U.S.A.

Text copyright © 2018 by Jacqueline J. Edgington
All rights reserved.

The Library of Congress has cataloged the hardcover edition: TX 8-671-040

First edition

ISBN-13   978-0-9980338-0-8

ISBN-10   0-9980338-0-4

For

Wayne

Amanda, Ceionna, Kearra & Kyla Raine

and especially for

Children of all ages searching for a way
home

Table of Contents

❧ CHAPTER 1 ❧

THE MONKEY PUZZLE TREE

"*Happy Jack, Happy Jack, run far away. Happy Jack, Happy Jack, don't you come back,*" were the words ringing in his ears.

Mounting the steps two at a time, he yanked open the big front door and ran right smack bang into the belly of Auntie Joyce.

"Oof! Jack! How many times have I told you not to run?"

He skirted around her and continued running up the two flights of stairs, wrenched open the bedroom door and dove onto his bed face down.

"I hate my school. I hate my auntie and uncle. And I hate my home," cried Jack out loud to whoever cared to hear him.

Jack lived with Auntie Joyce and Uncle Evan. That's what he was told to call them, even though they weren't really his auntie and uncle, and this wasn't really his home. Nothing was real anymore except for his tears. He felt them hot and wet as they rolled down his cheeks, soaking his pillow.

He didn't like crying like a big baby, but he couldn't stop. He sat up, grabbed his Rottweiler and threw him on the floor. He cried louder but he knew no one would come. No one ever came. He was a throwaway— thrown away just like he threw his dog on the floor.

This children's home was bigger than the last one he had lived in, and the kids were meaner. They called him Happy Jack because he never smiled. Happy Jack was the unhappiest boy in the whole world.

His new name followed him to school, and once a label sticks, you're tagged forever, until you move of course. In the last children's home, he was taunted with the label of Sad Sack Jack. He was moved out of that home because one of the older boys punched him in the face, giving him a bloody fat lip. Whenever he was moved to a new home, he always felt like he was being thrown away with his dog Ivanhoe. He was told by the grownups that the kids in this new home would be nicer and nearer to his age, but they always lied. There were no nine-year-olds here. They were all older than him, and they definitely weren't nice.

He looked down at Ivanhoe who stared right back up at him smiling. That's the thing about dogs: even if you're mean to them, they love you no matter what. As he picked Ivanhoe up off the floor, he saw the stitching coming loose around his ear. "I hope his ear won't fall off like his eye did," he thought to himself as small hiccups replaced his sobs.

He used the back of his dog to wipe away his tears. Perhaps that's why Ivanhoe's fur was all matted, but at least he was still soft. Jack couldn't remember where Ivanhoe had come from, but like a faithful dog, Ivanhoe had followed him wherever he went.

There was a scratch on the window by Jack's bed. He didn't dare look. He knew it was the huge scaly monster trying to get in. Jack got up and walked away from the window. He went past all the other beds, plopped down on the stool in front of the weathered dressing table and started opening and closing the drawers. There was nothing in them that belonged to him. All he had was his dog Ivanhoe and his tears. He looked into the large mirror and found himself staring miserably back. Happy Jack. The name suited him, he thought.

Two years ago, his mom had walked right out of the front door and never came back. His dad, without a word, dropped him off at the police station. His mom and dad had thrown him away. A big black hole had opened up, and he was living in it—Happy Jack and his dog Ivanhoe.

Jack continued to stare at himself in the mirror. The more he stared at his reflection, the lonelier he felt. So alone. So...nothing. He was nothing but an image. He didn't feel real anymore. He and his image stared at each other. It seemed as if he was frozen in time. He was fading into himself, disappearing into a big black hole called life. He shook himself as if from a bad dream and continued staring at his unsmiling reflection.

After a while, Jack got up and went into the garden with his books to do his homework. Ivanhoe accompanied him as they hid beneath the branches of the huge weeping willow tree that draped across the ground. He liked hiding there so the older kids could do their kid business without involving him. When he had finished his homework, he sat there chatting to his dog until he was called in for dinner.

"Jack," he heard Auntie Joyce calling. "Time to come in; dinner's ready."

Once the ordeal of dinner was over, the time came Jack dreaded the most. It was bedtime. In this home, his bedtime was at eight. He had to go to bed before all the older kids. On his way up the stairs, he would start to shrink and drag his feet. His bed was at the front of the house near the window, but no one would swap with him. This was the time the older kids called him, "Scaredy Cat Jack," followed by a chorus of meows. Scaredy Cat Jack was another label that had stuck because during the night, he became very scared. He couldn't stop his dreams. He would wake up in the middle of the night crying because a huge scaly monster would chase him in his sleep. He could never remember his dream when the morning came. He only remembered the feeling of being chased.

The huge scaly monster continued its scratching as if sharpening its claws on the window. It scratched louder at night as the dark stretched towards him. After pulling the curtains as tightly as he could, Jack lay in his bed. The curtains would never agree to meet so he could close out the monster. Jack couldn't help but see the searing white eyes looking in through the gaps. The starry, white-hot eyes appeared to be falling towards him, ready to burn.

When Jack woke up crying one night, waking up the other boys in turn, Uncle Evan came to his bed and told him there were no monsters trying to get in, but Jack would have none of it. He could still hear the scratching against the window as the wind moaned outside along with the awoken boys moaning inside. They were quickly shushed as Uncle Evan warned them not to rouse the whole house.

Uncle Evan patiently explained that it was only the tree outside and the wind moving the branches against the window. He assured Jack there were no eyes looking in. It was only the stars twinkling in the night sky. Uncle Evan smiled at him as he explained that the tree was called a *monkey puzzle tree*. It was named that long ago because when a man saw it for the first time growing in his friend's garden, he remarked that a monkey would be puzzled if it tried to climb it. Jack thought if he were a monkey, he wouldn't want to go near it. No way would he want to climb those sharp, scaly branches.

❧ CHAPTER 2 ❧

PETUCAN

"Wake up! Come on, Jack, wake up!" said a soft voice.

As he tossed and turned, his strawberry blond head sank deeper into his pillow.

"Jack, wake up! You're having another bad dream," urged the gentle voice.

8

Jack sat bolt upright in his bed. He could feel his face covered with sweat as he stared at the dark silhouette.

"Jack. Come on, wake up. It's only another dream."

He tried to shake off his bad dream and began to focus on the outline near his bed. He thought he was still dreaming. Instinctively, he knew it wasn't Uncle Evan. As his eyes adjusted, the image began to solidify and then it glowed a little. As it gently brightened, he could make out big ears framing a soft cotton face. He saw a button nose—seriously, it really was a button. There were large purple lips that smiled and a long tail peeking from behind the left side of the purple body. He looked into bright smiling eyes surrounded by thick eyebrows and a long mane of white hair. He realized he was looking at a very strange monkey.

"What, uh, who're you?" He trembled as he shook his head, still trying to wake up.

"Hello, Jack. My name is Petucan," answered the monkey.

Staring, he saw that the monkey wore a long-cotton shirt with one green sleeve and the other orange. The right side was yellow and the left side was red. The shirt had shiny buttons , and even though he couldn't see it, Jack was sure the back of the shirt was yellow.

The monkey's denim blue jeans spilled over large furry feet. Jack noticed all this in a blink of an eye. He moved back against his pillow. He wasn't sure if the monkey had climbed down from the monkey puzzle tree and come in through the window, but one thing was sure: there was a monkey standing by his bed. Perhaps he was still asleep in the throes of his nightmare. Jack became very still, afraid to blink, let alone move.

As Jack sat in his bed, he saw small sparkles of light begin to orbit the monkey like fireflies in a busy dance. The sparkles were all colors of the rainbow that managed to escape and melt into the shadows.

Always, since Jack could remember, he would wake in the night crying from bad dreams, and then he would be tired the next morning because he was afraid to go back to sleep. Now he was afraid because he thought he couldn't wake up. It felt like he was awake, but surely it must be a dream.

"It's okay, Jack. You're safe," said Petucan.

"You're not real," Jack accused. "GO AWAY!" he cried out loud, hoping to wake someone else up, not caring if they shouted at him.

"I'm real, Jack, and you're safe from your bad dream. There's nothing to worry about," said Petucan gently.

"But..." he didn't know what to say next to the talking monkey standing head and shoulders above the edge of his bed. It wasn't real, even though he could see it with his own eyes and hear it with his own ears. It couldn't be. He tried to shake his head again to wake himself up. He wanted to push the monkey away from him but didn't dare. He was afraid that somehow, the monkey would grow into the monster of his dreams and start chasing him when he ran. But right now, facing the talking monkey, he didn't have the nerve to run anywhere.

"I'm not your monster, Jack. I'm here to save you from your bad dreams," Petucan said as if he had read his thoughts.

"How?" Jack accused.

"Well, first you need a friend," answered Petucan.

"You're not my friend. I don't know you. Ivanhoe's my best friend," said Jack, still wishing the monkey would go away and he would wake up.

Petucan looked at the small stuffed dog, which had slid to the floor as Jack had tossed and turned in his bed. Jack watched as the monkey raised his hand and scattered rainbow dust all around the room, which began to sparkle and glow. None of the other kids stirred. They continued snoring soundly in their beds.

As the rainbow dust settled upon his dog, Ivanhoe began to get bigger and then lift his head. It was the magic rainbow dust that gave Jack's dog a voice. And with his deep voice, Jack's very best friend sang, "My master made claim and gave me my name. I thought you should know it is Ivanhoe."

Jack was astonished. Ivanhoe had never made a sound before. Not even a bark. He had always talked to his dog, especially when he was sad or angry, but Ivanhoe had only listened. Jack looked at Ivanhoe. Ivanhoe looked back with a smile.

"Um...hello, Ivanhoe," said Jack, sinking deeper into his pillow. He felt his nerves prick his skin. Then he almost shot out of bed when Ivanhoe began to shift towards him and jump up, landing on top of his legs.

Ivanhoe knew it was his job to look after his master. Every night, he had sat at the bottom of the bed and watched Jack fall asleep. But, nearly every night, Jack would toss and turn when one of his bad dreams visited him, and Ivanhoe would end up on the floor.

Feeling pinned to his bed with Ivanhoe on top and the monkey at his side, Jack had a weird feeling that he had met Petucan before, even though the memory escaped him. Something in the back of his mind also told him it wasn't the first time he had seen Ivanhoe come to life right before his very eyes. It seemed like he had been here before doing the exact same thing, only this time it felt a little different. Something was resting at the edge of his memory, but he couldn't recall what it was. Nervous and frightened, he sat in his bed feeling his palms sweat as he tried to remember. "Perhaps I've been watching too many movies," the thought popped in. He pinched himself so he could wake up. It hadn't been a hard pinch, but he felt it alright. He shook himself as if trying to shake away a dream. He wondered why none of the other kids had woken up. Surely, someone could hear him talking.

"How's this possible?" he silently asked himself. "A big talking monkey by my bed and my dog coming alive?" The remnants of his bad dream began to creep its way back in.

"It's really okay, Jack. I always wake you up when you're having a bad dream. It's just a dream and you're safe," said Petucan, who knew precisely that bad dreams were really good dreams and told Jack so. "I can help you," he continued.

"How's that?" Jack asked trying to settle himself.

Petucan asked Jack about his bad dream so he could explain why it was a good dream.

"I can't remember what I was dreaming about," he answered, not really wanting to remember but trying hard to remember whether he had met Petucan before.

"If you cannot remember your dreams, then you cannot find the good things," explained Petucan.

Talking to Petucan and hearing his gentle voice, Jack began to soften, and he pushed the bad dream away. Instinctively, he knew he was not in any danger. Strange as this dream was, he, Ivanhoe and Petucan talked about happy things while all the other kids slept on. Then they began to monkey around and play games until Jack tired and was ready to settle down for the night.

Jack fell safely back to sleep, and when he woke up the very next morning, he had forgotten all about his bad dream. He forgot about Petucan and the fact that Ivanhoe had sung to him.

After breakfast, Jack went off to school, dragging his feet behind the older kids so he could get some distance. During school, he always stuck close to the teachers, especially at lunch time. After school, he once again hid under the branches of the giant weeping willow tree that hung low in the backyard until he was called in for dinner. He had to sit with all the other kids at dinnertime and listen as they talked about things that didn't really interest him. Things like football, movies and who had the latest games on their phones.

But it was bedtime now. Jack never really knew why he didn't want to go to bed because he could never remember his bad dreams. As usual, he gave his Auntie Joyce a hard time when it was his turn to go to bed.

"You must get a good night's sleep, Jack," said Auntie Joyce as she patted him goodnight.

Jack's shoulders slumped as he trudged up the stairs. He ran the tap, pretending to wash and brush his teeth. He didn't like washing or brushing his teeth. He thought it was a waste of time, and he got away with it because no one checked on him in this home. As he crossed the room, he sat Ivanhoe at the bottom of his bed and shivered when he heard the sharp scratches on the window. After closing the curtains as best as he could, he climbed into bed and pulled the covers tightly under his chin.

"Wake up! Come on, Jack, wake up!" urged the soft voice.

15

Once again, Jack's strawberry blond hair was wet with sweat as he tossed and turned in his bed.

"Jack, wake up! You're having another bad dream."

Sitting bolt upright in his bed, Jack rubbed his soft blue eyes. His small freckled face turned towards the soft silhouette standing by his bed. Then he was surprised. He remembered. He remembered Petucan. He realized that Petucan always came to save him from his bad dreams. He'd never remembered before. How was it he remembered now?

"I wanted you to remember me, Jack. That way, you might remember your dreams and then I can help you," said Petucan to his unasked question.

The monkey raised his hand and scattered rainbow dust all around the room, making it sparkle and glow. As the rainbow dust rested upon Jack's ever faithful friend, Ivanhoe immediately jumped onto Jack's bed for a cuddle as he sung in his deep voice, "I'm Ivanhoe, but that you know. It makes me sad that your dreams are so bad."

"Oh Ivanhoe, don't worry about me. I have you and Petucan to keep me safe."

"But it would be great, and it's not too late, for you to learn why you toss and turn," sang Ivanhoe.

"It's true, Jack. If you learn what makes you have bad dreams, you won't have to toss and turn anymore," said Petucan in his soft monkey voice.

"I can't remember what I've been dreaming about, and I don't want to," huffed Jack.

"You don't have to remember, because we can go to Dhyāna Land," replied Petucan with a smile.

"Dhyāna Land? What's that?"

"Dhyāna Land is a very quiet place. It's a place where dreams are made," answered Petucan.

"I don't wanna go. Dreams scare me," whimpered Jack.

"But if you go to Dhyāna Land, you can learn to dream of anything you like. Your dreams don't have to be bad. I can show you," assured Petucan.

"How?" spouted Jack.

"I can guide you. There's a very big waterfall in Dhyāna Land. It's by the waterfall that Satya lives. Satya has the answer to all dreams because Satya is the dreamer of all dreams," answered Petucan.

"Who's Satya?" asked Jack. "I've never heard that name before."

"I'll introduce you. When you meet Satya, you'll find the answers to your bad dreams," replied Petucan.

Wanting to trust Petucan and get rid of his bad dreams, Jack asked, "How do we find the waterfall? How do we get to Dhyāna Land?"

"Close your eyes and think about a colorful waterfall. As soon as you imagine what it looks like, you will arrive," explained Petucan.

Jack thought about this. "Can Ivanhoe come too?"

"Of course," he answered as Ivanhoe's tail wagged furiously with delight.

❧ CHAPTER 3 ❧

DHYĀNA LAND

J ack closed his eyes and pictured a waterfall in his mind. It was as if he could hear a downpour splashing into a pool. He sensed the rushing water falling from a great height. He could feel the fresh, cold, misty spray against his small freckled face. He could feel the sun warming his body as the gentle breeze played with his hair. He felt the small stones moving beneath his slippers as the damp grass caressed his ankles.

When he opened his eyes, Jack looked at Petucan, who was smiling back at him. He looked at Ivanhoe by his side. He knew he was no longer sitting in his bed. Instead, he was standing in front of the waterfall that he had imagined in his mind.

Jack was suddenly afraid. He thought he was about to have another bad dream.

"There's nothing to be afraid of," said Petucan as he reassuringly wrapped his soft cotton fingers around Jack's hand.

"Am I dreaming or are we really here?" asked Jack, wondering why he felt okay holding hands with a cotton monkey.

"Dreams are real dreams," answered Petucan with a purple smile.

And with that, Ivanhoe sang in his deep voice, "Where are we. it's easy to see. As quick as a blink, we are where we think."

"Is Satya here?" asked Jack as he smiled down at Ivanhoe.

As soon as the word Satya was spoken, a soft light appeared in the midst of the waterfall creating the most brilliant rainbow Jack had ever seen. Such beautiful colors played in and out of the ripples and splashes. Jack was drawn to the soft white light like a moth to a flame. It didn't hurt his eyes as it pulsed gently like a heartbeat, expanding slowly towards him. In fact, Jack could not take his eyes off of it. As if in a trance, he stood and stared. It seemed like the light was calling to him, which is what made him reach out his hand to touch it.

Splash!

Into the waterfall Jack went. He had reached over just a little too far and toppled head first into the sparkling pool.

"Help! Help! I'm drowning!" cried Jack as he thrashed his arms around in panic.

Petucan and Ivanhoe stood on the bank and looked. Neither took a step to help him.

"HELP!" cried Jack at the top of his lungs.

"Stand up, Jack," urged Petucan.

Jack put down his foot and stood up. When he realized he was only knee-deep, he climbed out of the water feeling very foolish. Standing safely on the bank, he began wringing the water out of his pajamas. He was not happy at all being soaking wet, let alone hurting his pride in front of Petucan and Ivanhoe.

"I could've drowned if it'd been deeper," snapped Jack, trying to be angry at them instead of himself, even though he knew how to swim.

"How deep was the water?" asked Petucan.

Jack thought about this. He was not sure if he had stood on the bottom or not. When he had fallen in, the water had covered his head, but when he had stood up, the water was only knee-deep. He didn't really know how deep the pool of water was, but somehow, he knew he hadn't reached the bottom.

"It doesn't matter how deep it is. You still shouldn't have stood there looking at me. I would've helped you," spluttered Jack, feeling very embarrassed at having fallen in, "and Ivanhoe, you're supposed to protect me," he continued.

Ivanhoe bowed his head. He was not used to being scolded by his master, and in an even lower voice, he sang, "I'm sorry to laugh at you taking a bath. But as you can see, you're safe with Petucan and me."

Jack couldn't remember ever having been angry with Ivanhoe before. He'd been upset and thrown his stuffed dog on the floor out of frustration but it had never been Ivanhoe's fault. He had never blamed his dog for anything. Ivanhoe was the only friend he'd ever had.

"I'm sorry I told you off, Ivanhoe. I guess it was about time I took a bath." When suddenly, "Hey! I'm all dry! How did I get all dry?" he wondered out loud.

"Satya knew you were unhappy being all wet," explained Petucan. "Satya made you all dry. And whether you fall in or dive in, it's good to get wet now and again. If you never got wet, you'd never learn how to swim."

"Where is Satya?" asked Jack as he turned his head from side-to-side.

"Satya is here. You only have to look," replied Petucan.

Jack looked very hard indeed. He looked all around him. He looked up at the trees and around the big rocks. He looked down into the pool of water, but he only saw his reflection staring back at him.

"I still can't see Satya," said Jack.

"Then perhaps you are not ready to see," Petucan continued. "The quieter you are, the easier it is to see."

Jack thought about this. He'd spent plenty of time sitting quietly under the weeping willow tree but had never seen Satya. He wanted to meet Satya, the dreamer of all dreams. "Can you help me look?" he asked.

Petucan smiled. "Let's go and visit Patrick the leprechaun. He can guide you to a very quiet place. Then you can meet Satya."

"A leprechaun? I've never met a leprechaun before. Where does Patrick live?"

"Oh, not very far from here. There's a sandcastle on the beach about one hundred and eight miles away. That's where we'll find Patrick," he answered smiling at the surprise on Jack's face.

"A hundred and eight miles!" Jack repeated. "That's a very long way. How do we get there?" he asked.

"The same way we got to the waterfall," replied Petucan. "Just think of a sandy beach with a very big sandcastle."

❧❦ CHAPTER 4 ❧❦

THE GIANT SANDCASTLE

No sooner had the thought popped into his head, Jack found himself face-to-face with a very big sandy door. As he looked around, he could see the foamy waves rolling along the coast. Seagulls played in and out of the surf as turtles scurried for the open sea.

Jack turned back towards the sandcastle. It was completely made of sand from top to bottom.

"Wow, that's the biggest sandcastle I've ever seen," exclaimed Jack, "but it's not as big as a regular house."

"A house is a house," said Petucan simply.

Upon hearing these words, Ivanhoe stopped running in the sand and began to sing in his deep voice, "Behind a quiet door you're safe and secure. When you turn your key, you can sit and be."

Jack patted his best friend and ran his hand over the bumpy brown fur. Before Petucan could stop him, Jack turned around and boldly knocked upon the sandy door. The bold knock rippled throughout the door as the walls started to vibrate from front to back. The roof shook and soon the whole sandcastle was swaying back-and-forth and from side-to-side.

"Quick, run!" cried Petucan.

Jack ran from the shaking sandcastle with Ivanhoe in his wake. Petucan was not far from their side. They all turned their heads just in time to see the whole sandcastle collapse into a big sandy heap. As fast as he could, Jack ran back to the big pile of sand and fell to his knees digging hurriedly with his bare hands.

"QUICK, HELP ME!" shouted Jack.

Petucan and Ivanhoe stood watching Jack as he continued to dig desperately into the sand with both hands.

"What are you doing?" asked Petucan.

"Patrick is buried in the sand. We have to dig him out. Please help," pleaded Jack.

"How do you know he was home?" asked Petucan with a smile.

Before Jack could even think about it, he heard a very cheerful laughing song coming along the shore. As he squinted his eyes in the sunlight, he could make out a tiny figure jauntily walking towards them.

The song grew louder as the figure got closer.

"Well, well, well. What'er we 'ere den?" asked the small rounded figure in a strange accent. The strange accent matched the strange clothes the leprechaun wore. Patrick had on bright yellow pants with fat blue suspenders holding them up. The fat blue suspenders lay over a pink and green polka-dot shirt. He wore a black top hat with a large red Christmas bow on the front. Shiny silver buckles graced his brown leather shoes. All in all, he didn't seem like the typical leprechaun one read about in a children's book.

Jack looked very afraid as he searched the red-cheeked face for sympathy. After all, it had been an accident. It had never crossed his mind that the sandcastle would fall down when he knocked on the sandy door. Instead of answering, Jack sat down and began to cry. He felt so guilty that he had knocked down the leprechaun's home.

Ivanhoe licked the salty tears from Jack's face. He didn't like to see his master so unhappy. It made him unhappy too.

"I'm s' s' sorry," stuttered Jack through his sobs, blaming himself for the home falling apart.

"Now, now den young man, stop yer cryin'. Ders no real damage dat 'er done," said the leprechaun.

With that, Patrick started to laugh. In fact, he laughed so hard, he had to hold on to his large round belly to stop it from shaking. He laughed and laughed. Soon, his whole body quivered with laughter.

The laughing was infectious. Ivanhoe began to snuffle and snort then rolled in the sand barking out laughs. Unable to help himself, Petucan began to titter with laughter, which got louder and louder.

Jack, who normally had a hard time smiling let alone laughing, could not believe his eyes and ears. He stood back up and looked from the leprechaun to Petucan and then to Ivanhoe listening to their chorus of laughter.

"What could be so funny? Are they laughing at me or the knocked-down sandcastle?" he asked himself. "Am I having a good dream or a bad dream?" he asked out loud.

It was a long time before they could all stop laughing and a very long time before Jack's question was answered.

"We ain't laughin' at you, me sonny boy," said the leprechaun. "Ain't nice to laugh at nobody," he continued.

"Then what's so funny?" asked Jack as he wiped the tears from his face feeling a little better.

"Tis good to laugh. Yer gotta laugh and laugh out loud," said the leprechaun. "You can cry if you want to but laughin's better."

"But your home. It's fallen down. It's all gone," said a confused Jack.

"Dat der 'ouse ain't me 'ome, sonny boy. You'll ne'r trap me in an 'ouse. And anyways, what youngen doesn't like knockin' down sandcastles? It's every boy's dream t' knock down a giant sandcastle. I 'av a lot o' fun buildin' 'em and knockin' 'em down. If I didn't knock 'em down, the tide 'll take 'em. Nothin' lasts ferever."

"Then where do you live?" asked Jack very much relieved.

"Me, sonny boy, lives in a very quiet place where de silence is me windows," answered the leprechaun.

"Oh! Do you mean the quiet place that I'm looking for?" asked Jack. "Petucan told me about it. Is it the same place where Satya lives?"

"Me beloved Satya. So dat's what yer 'ere fer. To find Satya," stated Patrick as if he already knew.

"Can you tell me which way to go to find the quiet place?" asked Jack.

"Course I can. I live dere, don't I? You don't 'ave to go far. All you 'ave to do is be quiet," answered the leprechaun simply.

"Be quiet?" thought Jack to himself. "I'm always quiet."

It was the quietness that helped make Jack invisible so he wasn't picked on. If the bullies couldn't hear him, he could become so small they wouldn't notice him and chase him. It was easy for Jack to be quiet. The quietness was his escape. But Jack had never ever tried to be quiet when the bullies weren't around. That's when he would talk to Ivanhoe, out of earshot of the other kids so they wouldn't think he was dumb. He certainly didn't need to give them any more excuses to pick on him. Quietness was his natural defense but sometimes, it was not enough to be quiet. Sometimes, the bullies could see through the quietness and then in one long chant as they chased him, he would hear, "Happy Jack, Happy Jack, run far away. Happy Jack, Happy Jack, don't you come back."

Perhaps this was just a silly dream after all, but at least right now, he wasn't being chased by bullies. Jack decided he had nothing to lose because he had already lost everything. He decided he would be quiet so he could try and find the quiet place.

"How long do I have to be quiet for?" he asked.

"You'll 'ave to be quiet fer as long as it takes, sonny boy. If yer can't be quiet, yer can't find the quiet place. If yer can't find the quiet place, yer can't find Satya," answered the leprechaun.

Even though he thought this was a silly dream, Jack wanted to find the quiet place, so he could meet Satya, the dreamer of all dreams. He thought he would try anything or go to anyone who could help him put an end to all of his nightmares. So, Jack became very quiet. He never spoke a word.

❦ CHAPTER 5 ❦

MONKEY MIND

Jack had a hard time listening to the quiet. He could still hear the sea. He could hear the wind. He could hear all the thoughts that came popping into his head. His thoughts began to argue with themselves. One thought said he was stupid and told him to wake up. Another thought told him to stay asleep because then he could avoid the bullies in the real world. Another thought told him this world was as real as any other world, and another thought told him he should run away from the real world because there was only unhappiness living there.

The harder Jack concentrated on being quiet, the louder his thoughts screamed in his head, bickering and throwing words at each other. Jack thought his head was about to explode.

"STOP," shouted Jack.

His mind wouldn't shut up. Not for a second. It was like a cacophony of monkeys all screeching at one another inside his head.

"Jack, Jack, it's okay," assured Petucan as he gently shook him.

Jack hadn't realized he'd closed his eyes, and when he opened them, he was shocked to find himself standing under a great big tree. To his horror, the tree was the same monkey puzzle tree that stood right outside his bedroom window as if barring any escape. Looking up, he saw that the tree had grown. It was over a hundred feet tall, and Jack knew the tree was looking down at him. He looked at the branch right by his face. He saw the thick, tough, scaly leaves. They were fat triangles with sharp-tipped edges aimed at his eyes. The noise in his head hadn't stopped. As Jack looked around, he saw that the tree was surrounded by hundreds of small chattering monkeys. He took a step back and quickly turned away, running as fast as he could run, not caring if he stepped on their tails.

Petucan and Ivanhoe ran after him crying for him to stop. It was only when Jack got a stitch in his side that he collapsed on the jungle floor.

"A jungle?" Jack exclaimed. "I'm in a jungle! This isn't a quiet place! It's a JUNGLE!"

Petucan and Ivanhoe caught up and flopped to the ground next to Jack.

"A jungle!" accused Jack as he looked at Petucan. "The monkey puzzle tree!" he cried. "What am I doing here?"

And in his deep voice came the reply, "It's not such a puzzle when your thoughts are a-muzzle. You had to take flight because you can't sit and be quiet."

"Ivanhoe, that's not fair. There were monkeys fighting in my head and now I'm in a jungle with a monster monkey puzzle tree surrounded by hundreds of screeching monkeys that won't shut up," cried Jack. "I bet even those monkeys are afraid to climb that tree," he finished.

In answer, Ivanhoe sang in his deep voice, "You will see it's only a tree. Over one thousand years, it's heard all the tears."

"What do you mean?" asked Jack.

Petucan explained that the monkey puzzle tree had stood for over a thousand years. Even the thick juicy leaves lasted for over twenty-five years before new growth appeared. The monkeys would gather around the base of the tree because its top was like a big umbrella. The monkeys could sit in the shade and cool down.

"But there are lots of trees in the jungle. Why'd the monkeys pick that one if they can't climb it?" asked Jack.

"It's a special tree because it's a rare puzzle tree," answered Petucan. "And because the monkeys like to monkey around it," he continued.

"What's so special about it? Now I'm puzzled."

"When the monkeys want to know something, they think about what it is they want to know. They do this while sitting under the monkey puzzle tree, and the tree puzzles out their thoughts. That's how they learn what to do and how to live. The monkeys call it the 'Tree of All-Knowing.'"

As Jack looked back in the direction he had ran from, he could see the tree standing tall and proud. It was almost majestic as it towered above the canopy of the jungle. Jack could see the sun as it sparkled between the thick rubbery leaves, even at this distance.

Ivanhoe looked in the same direction and sang in his deep voice, "The tree would be kind and read your mind. Unless it's no matter if your mind is a-chatter."

"Of course, it matters, Ivanhoe. If Jack can't be quiet, especially with his monkey mind all a-chatter, he won't find the quiet place and can't meet Satya," Petucan responded.

"I'm scared," said Jack. "I'm worried in case the tree wants to hurt me. It's very big and sharp and it frightens me."

"The leaves are only sharp so the tree can protect itself. It protects itself from the chattering monkeys. That's how it's stood for a thousand years. All of nature protects itself especially from humans who tend to rip into it without thinking of the consequences. Nature has a way of fighting back. But you don't have to worry, because this particular tree is a very rare puzzle tree. It will help you. It will stand and listen and then help solve the puzzles in your head. Once you tell it your fears and your worries, then your fears won't be so worrisome," explained Petucan.

As Jack looked at the tree once more, it seemed to stand with grandeur just like the toy dinosaurs on his bedside table. He'd often imagined riding on the back of a dinosaur, crashing through a jungle, slashing his sword as the bullies ran out of his way.

"Let's go back to the monkey puzzle tree and find out why your mind can't be quiet," suggested Petucan.

Jack agreed, albeit a little reluctantly, and off the three went, heading back to the circle of chattering monkeys that surrounded the giant tree. Upon closer inspection, the thick bark looked weathered and almost charred. There were long cucumber-shaped cones and other cones that were round and fat. Petucan explained that the tree was like a living fossil and that particular species of tree had been around since the time of the dinosaurs.

"I knew it!" said Jack looking at the reptile scale leaves that wrapped their way around the thick branches. "But what're those?" he asked pointing.

"They're cones that produce seeds, which you can eat. The long ones are male and the round ones are female."

That made Jack giggle, and then he looked down because he thought he was being rude. He could tell Petucan knew what he was smiling at.

"It's nice to see you smile, Jack," said Petucan.

Jack couldn't understand why he suddenly felt he had been caught out. Quickly changing the subject, he asked, "How come the tree has boy cones and girl cones?"

"Sometimes, that happens in nature. Sometimes, a monkey puzzle tree will produce both male and female cones," answered Petucan.

Jack couldn't help snickering and voiced some of the words he had learnt in the children's home.

"Jack," admonished Petucan, "you know how you feel when people call you names. Nature, buy its very name, is natural. Look how tall and proud this tree stands, and that's not all; it inspires the monkeys to be kind to each other. That's why they like this tree so much. It teaches them to stop fighting amongst themselves."

"I guess it's not a monster after all," said Jack a little chastised. "It's a monster of a tree an' all, but I don't think it wants to hurt me. It'd hurt a monkey's hands and feet though if a monkey tried to climb it," he continued as he looked around at the gaily chattering monkeys.

"Monkeys are smarter than you think. That's why you don't see them trying to climb it. Monkeys just want to learn. That's why they chatter so much. If they don't understand what they're learning, they argue continuously," explained Petucan. "They come to this tree because it's so old. They share their thoughts with the monkey puzzle tree until the answers come to them. The tree helps them puzzle out their questions. It's the oldest tree in the jungle. It's been around since before the monkeys, so it knows how the monkeys came to exist. It helps the monkeys look back so they can then look forward. If you don't have a history, then you can't have a future."

With these words, the fear started to creep up Jack's legs. He could feel the fear settle into his body slithering to the tips of his fingers and crawling to the top of his head. The hair at the back of his neck began to stand up. He felt the rays of the sun prick his skin as they darted through the leaves.

"I want to leave now," complained Jack.

Ivanhoe whined as he smelt the fear emanating from his master. Even though he was ready to fight, his tail curled between his legs.

"Why are you afraid?" asked Petucan.

"I don't wanna look back," answered Jack. "That's where nightmares live."

"If you can't see your past, you can't look to your future," stated Petucan. "You'll always be living in limbo. There's nothing to worry about, Jack. You're safe with me and Ivanhoe."

"What makes you so sure?" asked Jack.

"Because the past is in the pages of your memory, and the future hasn't happened. There is only now, Jack. Just this very moment. Don't you feel safe right now?"

Doubt began to lodge itself in Jack's head. "You're a liar. Just like everyone else. Everyone says I'm safe and things will get better, but they don't. They only get worse," he accused. "No one tells the truth. No one cares. No one wants me. My mom didn't want me. My dad didn't want me. All the other kids don't wanna play with me. They bully me and call me names. I hate it. I hate it. I hate this jungle. I hate this dream and I HATE MONKEYS!"

The words vomited out of Jack's mouth as he fell to the ground sobbing, hiccupping and gasping for breath. He felt like he was dying. He felt sick. Sick of being afraid. Sick of running. Just sick.

It seemed like eons had passed when Jack raised his head. He felt empty, as if poison had been lanced from his body. The emptiness was almost sweet. His sour words had spewed forth along with his bad memories. The memories hung in the air. Memories of his past. Memories of a door slamming. Memories of a police officer taking him by the hand.

The monkeys looked on without a sound. Even the chattering in his mind had gone. There was just a pleasant quiet calm. It was as if the calm was caressing him from the inside.

As Jack looked at the monkeys, a young one came gingerly towards him, stretched out its hand and offered him a banana. Jack looked into the deep, velvety eyes of the young monkey, and realized he was hungry. He peeled the banana and ate it gratefully, patting the monkey on the head. Then, as banana after banana were offered to him by the other monkeys, he ate another and another. No matter how many bananas he ate, he still felt hungry. There was something more Jack needed. Something was missing.

"The monkey puzzle tree has absorbed your bad memories. It's heard your words and read your thoughts. It will keep your memories, just like history is stored with words in a book. The monkey puzzle tree feeds off history good and bad, happy or sad. Trees are record keepers and this particular tree has more records than any other living tree. If trees disappeared, there will be no records to tell that we even existed. There will be no present, no past and therefore no future," explained Petucan.

Jack felt as if he'd been massaged on the inside with calmness, or was it the bananas sliding down his belly? He took a deep breath and felt the pain leave as he exhaled. He was no longer afraid of the monkey puzzle tree. He wanted to hug it and he did just that. The trunk was so large, his hands didn't meet. He felt the warmth seeping from the rough bark into his body. He felt as if he had made a friend. He realized then that he was not alone. He had Ivanhoe, Petucan and the monkey puzzle tree. The monkeys, having witnessed another puzzle beginning to unravel, smiled up at him as they gently rose and walked happily back into the foliage of the jungle, disappearing one-by-one.

It was the first time Jack had spoken about his past, albeit in rage, fear and blame. When he looked at Petucan and Ivanhoe, he knew he could trust them. He knew they wouldn't judge him, ridicule him and call him names. He knew it with all his heart. And his heart grew warm.

"What do we do now?" asked Jack, looking around. "Can we still find the quiet place?"

"Of course, we can. There's a cosmic blueprint that lives in all things. That's how we can find anything we want to, even if it tries to hide from us. We all have a map within us to wherever we want to go. This universal map guides the birds so they know how to fly south. It guides the flowers so they face towards the sun. The rivers of life follow the map so they can become one with the ocean. But, where do you want to go? What is it that you really want, Jack?" asked Petucan.

Jack thought about this. "I don't want anything," he replied. "I just... I just wish..."

"What do you wish, Jack?" prompted Petucan.

"I wish my mom and dad hadn't thrown me away." There, he said it, but only to himself. Jack had always wished for a family—a normal family with a mom and dad. Maybe even a sister.

"I just wish. That's all," he snapped.

"We're in Dhyāna Land, Jack. You can dream for a wish."

"Really?" thought Jack. "I can dream for a wish and my wish will come true?" he asked out loud.

"What will come true is exactly what you wish for," answered Petucan.

Jack was skeptical, and even though he trusted Petucan, he couldn't admit what he truly wished for, especially in this strange place. Anything could happen, and he believed that nothing good would happen. Two years ago, his whole life had been turned upside down. His whole world had fallen apart with the slamming of a door. He secretly wished the door had never slammed. He secretly wished for his mom and dad.

"So, what do you wish for, Jack?" asked Petucan breaking into his thoughts.

Wishing his mom and dad had never left him; he stayed tight lipped. He wanted to hope that what Petucan said was true. He wanted to make a wish. But he also knew deep down that if you told someone your wish, it wouldn't come true. You had to keep a wish to yourself.

"Don't you have a wish?" asked Petucan.

"I might," answered Jack with a sullen voice. Then more forcibly than he meant to, "Yes, I do. I DO have a wish," he said taking them all by surprise.

"Why don't you make your wish now?" prompted Petucan.

Jack's longing for a family overcame his doubt. He closed his eyes picturing his wish, hoping his wish would come true. He tried and he tried, squeezing his eyes hard enough so they began to water. But for all he was worth, he couldn't remember what his mom and dad had looked like. He couldn't remember their faces, no matter how hard he tried. In fact, the harder he concentrated, the more distant the image became until there was nothing but a teary blur.

A sob caught in his throat as he opened his eyes. He wiped away a tear with the back of his hand before it had a chance to fall. But as he opened his mouth to tell Petucan he couldn't make a wish, he closed it. He found he was no longer standing in a jungle. He stood in a small meadow of bright-colored wildflowers. Petucan and Ivanhoe stood by his side wagging their tails with delight.

"Is this what you wished for?" asked Petucan hopping around. "This is a very nice place."

Jack looked around without answering. There were trees surrounding the edge of the meadow that were of all different shapes and sizes. He'd never seen so many. The grass in the meadow was lush and rippled like waves in the gentle breeze. The sun shone down as clouds drifted blissfully across the day like a paint brush offering shade.

Amazed and a little disoriented, Jack asked, "What's this place?"

"Perhaps you wished to be here," answered Petucan.

"No," he responded. "I wanted a wish, but I don't know where this is. I wanted a wish but couldn't picture it in my head," he said, still not wanting Petucan to know his secret wish.

"Even though you couldn't picture what it is you wanted, you did want a wish. Perhaps this is where you'll find a wish," replied Petucan as if a wish were a thing you could carry around with you.

And in his deep voice, Ivanhoe sang, "You wanted a wish because something's amiss. A mom and a dad so you won't be so sad."

"Well, I guess the dog's out of the bag now. Now you both know my wish," said Jack a little peeved. "I do want my mom and dad back so I can have a real home and be like the other kids at school. I don't want to bounce around anymore. It's not fair," admitted Jack turning away as the sadness started to creep back in when, "Oops... Whoa... Ouch." Jack had landed on all fours. "Dang, what was that?"

Jack sat up and spotted a rusty handle sticking out of the ground. "So, that's what I tripped over," he said pointing as he got back to his feet. He drew his foot back to kick it out of the way.

"Stop," cried Petucan. "It's a lamp."

"It's a rusty teapot. Someone must've dropped it. Perhaps they were having a picnic," said Jack.

"You can't make a cup of tea in the middle of a meadow. That's just plain silly," said Petucan. "I'm sure it's a lamp. It's not round like a teapot and its spout is very long."

Jack picked up the lamp. It was rusty. Really, really rusty.

❧ CHAPTER 6 ❧

WISH UPON A GENIE

"Ish bish, bish bosh, skiddle-dee-dee and skiddle-dee-do, make your wish now for it to come true," spoke the larger-than-life genie.

"Dong," went the little rusty oil lamp.

The genie had whooshed right out of the spout of the little lamp. He was ten feet tall with large laughing eyes and an even larger smiling smile. Jack had been trying to polish the rust and dirt off with his pajama sleeve and had jumped out of his skin dropping the little lamp.

"Hey! Watch out! That's my home you just dropped. Now I will have to tidy up when I go back in," said the genie. "What were you doing with my home anyway? Oh wait, let me guess. You were trying to polish it. Why does everyone have to polish my home? I like it just the way it is, thank you very much," he continued without waiting for an answer.

Jack, eyes wide, stared speechless at the large genie hovering in the air. The ebony-skinned genie had Bantu knots sitting atop his head and thick pearl and sandalwood beaded braids that snaked around him, caressing his tattooed arms as if they had a life of their own. Lying around his neck was a huge necklace made from giant rudraksha seeds with a gold tassel dangling at the center. On his left arm he wore a thick gold armband emblazoned with seven large gemstones of red, orange, yellow, green, blue, indigo and violet. The gemstones lit up, harmonizing, creating a mesmerizing silent beat. Jack had to tear his eyes away.

"Well, make your wish now. If you wish to be able to talk, just nod your head up and down and your wish will come true," the genie went on enticing Jack to meet his eyes.

Still speechless, Jack continued staring at the genie with his mouth agape as if his words feared what would happen should they emerge.

In the next instant, the genie whooshed back into the little rusty oil lamp leaving a sky-blue-pink misty trail behind.

Jack shook his head as if to wake himself up. "Impossible," he said out loud. He slowly bent down and picked up the little lamp. He looked at Petucan then at Ivanhoe who began to fidget. He gazed at the lamp in his hands. Very carefully, he examined it from top to bottom. All he saw were small sparkles that glinted out between the rust. As Petucan and Ivanhoe stood watching, he shook the little lamp. Nothing. Not even a rattle could be heard. He looked down the dark spout. Nothing. He turned the little lamp upside down to see if anything would fall out. Nothing.

"Perhaps my imagination's getting the better of me," said Jack to himself. He was beginning to feel a little silly. Petucan kept quiet but a low rumble could be heard coming from Ivanhoe. Once again, Jack tried to clean the rust off the little lamp.

"Ish bish, bish bosh, skiddle-dee-dee and skiddle-dee-do, make your wish now for it to come true," said the genie in a voice that was deep enough to fall into.

"Dong," went the little rusty oil lamp as it once again bounced on the ground.

"Hey! I've just tidied my home from the last time you dropped it. Now it's a total mess and everything is turned upside down," said the genie.

Again, wide eyed and speechless, Jack stood and stared.

"Speechless again? Oh well," sighed the genie as it whooshed back into the little lamp leaving a sky-blue-pink misty trail behind.

Suddenly, full of life as if waking from a dream, Jack picked up the little lamp. He was so excited because this was the first genie he had ever met. Holding the little lamp tightly, Jack gently rubbed the side.

"Ish bish, bish bosh, skiddle-dee-dee and skiddle-dee-do, make your wish now for it to come true," said the genie.

"Dong," went the little lamp as it bounced on the ground.

"Oh no, not again," complained the genie. "Now I have to tidy my home up yet again."

"I'm sorry," said Jack. "You make me jump when you whoosh out of your lamp."

"He speaks! And about time too!" said the genie. "Perhaps you can make your wish now so I can get back to playing with my friends."

"I didn't know you had friends in the lamp with you," said Jack.

"I don't," he replied. "I go to Genieland and meet all the other genies and generally have a good time playing genie tricks. So, what's your wish then?"

"I don't have a wish yet. I just wanted to introduce myself," answered Jack, feeling as if he'd been put on the spot.

"Why?" asked the genie with mirth in his eyes.

"Because it's good manners," answered Jack smiling back.

"Hello, I'm the genie of the lamp and you're Jack. I'm delighted to meet your acquaintance," he said bowing low.

"Hello," said Jack, amused at the cheeky genie who made him laugh in his cheeky way.

"Okay, introduction over. Do you have a wish?" he asked.

Jack, still stalling because he couldn't remember what his mom and dad had looked like, asked, "Can Petucan and Ivanhoe have a wish too?"

"Sorry. No can do. Only one wish per person. The person who rubs the lamp before it disappears. Very strict rules I'm afraid," answered the genie as his snaky thick braids nodded up and down in agreement.

"But I can't remember what to wish for. I can't remember my mom and dad or what they looked like," said Jack.

He instinctively knew his wish had to be thought about very carefully since only one wish was allowed and he wanted exactly what he had lost. He wanted his mom and dad.

"Oh well, when you do, just rub," sighed the genie as it whooshed back into the little rusty oil lamp leaving a sky-blue-pink misty trail behind.

"What a weird genie. I wonder if he has a special name," said Jack thinking aloud. And so once again he rubbed the side of the little lamp.

"Ish bish, bish bosh, skiddle-dee-dee and skiddle-dee-do, make your wish now for it to come true," said the genie flashing brilliant white teeth as if he knew what would happen next.

"Dong," went the little rusty oil lamp as it hit the ground.

"Again!" cried the genie without losing his grin. "Do you enjoy bouncing my home on the ground? Now I will have to tidy up for the fourth time today."

Jack apologized again, explaining that he wasn't used to all the whooshing and that it made him jump when he whooshed out of the lamp.

"Apology accepted. So, what's your wish then?" asked the genie slapping one of his errant braids that was trying to chase a blue winged flutterby.

The seven-winged flutterby resembled a butterfly and was the size of a small bird. The odd wing was centered at the tail end and acted like a rudder to help the flutterby dodge the genie's unruly braids.

"I only wanted to ask you if you have a special name," stated Jack.

"Why?" asked the genie.

"Because if there are lots of other genies, it would be nice to know your name," he replied.

"Why?" asked the genie with a playful smile.

"Well, um, because it's better than not knowing your name?" questioned Jack as Petucan started to giggle at the truculent genie.

"Why?" asked the genie yet again, almost laughing.

Jack could not believe his ears. He did not know what to say next. Even though he made him laugh, he wished the genie would be serious and answer his questions instead of just saying, "why" all the time. He decided to ask the genie another question.

"I know," said Jack to the genie, "why do you say the words, 'Ish bish, bish bosh, skiddle-dee-dee and skiddle-dee-do' when you whoosh out of your lamp?"

"Why not?" replied the genie this time laughing out loud.

With a sigh, Jack gave up. He wanted more time to think about his wish, leaving the genie to whoosh back into the little rusty oil lamp leaving a sky-blue-pink misty trail behind.

Jack knew he could wish for anything, but a mom and a dad were the only wish he really wanted. It was then that he realized his dilemma. *What happens if I can only wish for a mom or a dad? What if I can't have both with only one wish?* He decided to ask the genie. Holding very tightly onto the lamp, Jack rubbed the side with his hand.

"Ish bish, bish bosh, skiddle-dee-dee and skiddle-dee-do, make your wish now for it to come true," said the genie.

Jack still jumped but held onto the little lamp. "Can I have a mom and a dad with only one wish?" he asked.

"You already have a mom and dad," the genie answered reasonably. "If you didn't, you wouldn't be here. Everyone has a mom and dad."

"I don't," said Jack. "They left me. They didn't want me." And it was then that Jack tossed the lamp to the ground as the genie whooshed back inside.

"Jack!" said Petucan alarmed.

Sideling up to his side, "Don't get mad 'cause you're feeling so sad. You don't have to hate 'cause you can't control fate," sang Ivanhoe rubbing Jack's legs with his soft, cold nose.

This made Jack slump to the ground with his hands around his knees and his head buried between them. Not only did his parents throw him away, he couldn't picture them anymore. It was as if they were nothing more than a figment of his imagination. Why should he want them if they didn't want him? Why should he care if they didn't care about him? Why should he cry over them since they willingly gave him away? He felt Petucan's hand on his shoulder.

"GO AWAY," he shouted with tears ready to spill. "What's the use of having a wish? My mom and dad didn't want me. What was I thinking?"

"Jack, it's okay to cry. It's okay to miss not having parents," soothed Petucan.

"They didn't love me. And, I don't love anyone," cried an angry Jack.

"Look at Ivanhoe. You love him, don't you?" asked Petucan. "And Ivanhoe loves you very much. He's followed you everywhere."

"Ivanhoe's not real. This is just a silly dream. He's just a stuffed dog and you're a stuffed monkey. In fact, why don't you both get stuffed? Go away! Leave me alone!"

"Jack, didn't I tell you dreams were real? If your dream is real, then we are real too, stuffed or not."

"I wanna wake up now," demanded Jack.

"But what about your wish?" asked Petucan.

In a smaller than usual deep voice, Ivanhoe sang, "A dream's a dream, so know I don't mind. I know your heart and I know you are kind. So dry your face, put your heart back in place. Your kindness is love wrapped around a big hug."

Jack immediately put his arms around Ivanhoe and hugged him. "I'm sorry, Ivanhoe. I didn't mean to take it out on you. I'm sorry Petucan, I didn't mean to tell you to get stuffed."

"It's okay, Jack. I'm already stuffed," said Petucan with a smile.

Not for the first time, Ivanhoe dried Jack tears away as Jack buried his face in his soft lumpy fur.

"You are kind, Jack. You might run away from bullies and you might miss having a mom and dad, but you've never hurt anyone on purpose, even when they've hurt you," said Petucan as he looked up spotting some rooftops in the distance. "I know, let's go over there," he said pointing. "I can see a small village not too far away. There will be people there so we can get something to eat. I'm hungry. We can help someone in exchange for food. I'm sure there is something we can do. Let's see if we can be kind, then you'll feel better. Being kind always makes people feel better," advised Petucan.

Jack, giving up on wishing he had a mom and dad, agreed to go to the village nestling on the nearby hill. With a heavy heart and heavy footsteps, he walked with Petucan on one side and Ivanhoe on the other. The little rusty lamp was safely tucked under his arm as the three headed toward the small village. The further they walked, the more Jack thought about being kind. By the time they reached the path leading into the village, Jack decided that he would use his magic wish out of kindness. With the thought of being kind, he began to feel a little better. As they passed the village store, they came across a lady pushing a baby stroller with one hand and carrying bags of shopping with the other. The lady said hello and introduced herself as Mrs. Peters.

"Hello, Mrs. Peters," said Jack. "Would you like some help?"

"Thank you. It would be very helpful if you could carry these bags," replied Mrs. Peters.

Jack wanted to be kind and help her and knew they could all carry the bags between them. He wanted to save the wish for someone who needed a genie's special help.

After they left Mrs. Peters' house full of chocolate chip cookies and homemade lemonade, they came across a man who introduced himself as Mr. Ramirez. Mr. Ramirez was painting a fence bright blue.

"Would you like some help?" asked Jack.

"Why, thank you. It would be wonderful if you could help me paint this fence," answered Mr. Ramirez.

Jack smiled and thought he would enjoy painting the fence. Also, he would be able to save the wish for someone who needed more help that only a magic wish could bring. As Ivanhoe stirred the paint with a stick between his jaw, Jack and Petucan hummed a happy song as they painted the fence with Mr. Ramirez.

Once the fence was finished, Jack decided now was the perfect time to make his wish. He wanted the wish to make a difference. He wanted the wish to be helpful. He wanted to make someone happy. He also decided the only way to make a good wish was to sit down. He found the perfect spot by a lotus pond that rested in the middle of the park. As he sat down, he became quiet. His chattering monkey-mind calmed and his thoughts cleared. He sat crossed-legged with his hands on his knees and the lamp in his lap. Petucan and Ivanhoe sat down beside him. He felt at ease with his friends by his side. He closed his eyes and softened his breath. He was so much happier now because he had been kind and helpful all day. The people he had helped shone with love and kind words. The kindness moved through him and in no time at all, Jack knew what to wish for. In the next heartbeat, he jumped to his feet. He glowed with joy as he rubbed the side of the little lamp.

"Ish bish, bish bosh, skiddle-dee-dee and skiddle-dee-do, make your wish now for it to come true," said the genie.

"Dong," went the little lamp as it again bounced on the ground. Jack had forgotten to hold on to it tightly.

"How did I guess it was you, Jack? Perhaps I shall make you so small you can enter my lamp and tidy up my home since you have made it untidy again," chuckled the genie as it waved a finger like an upside-down pendulum.

Jack laughed as he said, "Once again, I'm sorry. The loud whooshing sound you make when you go in and out of your lamp still makes me jump."

The genie laughed with him. "Yes, I suppose it is a bit dramatic. So, have you a wish yet?"

"Yes," answered Jack.

"Finally!" exclaimed the genie.

With warmth in his heart, Jack beamed at the genie. "When your lamp is ever dropped, I wish for your home to always stay tidy," he wished.

"Genius! Just genius!" exclaimed the genie bowing deeply. "How wonderful and kind you are. No one has ever made a wish for me before." And the genie, hair ablaze with excitement, sang, danced, clapped and rapped:

"You don't need a wish to find a map,

There's a map, Happy Jack, namaste y'all.

Just follow the map and don't look back,

There's nothing you lack 'cause you're Happy Jack,
namaste y'all.

You can shove right back if spirit you lack,

Hold on and be quiet, namaste y'all.

Fighting you back are memories intact,

You can trash 'em or receive a lesson in compassion,

Oh, Happy Jack, namaste y'all.

So, live your life 'cause you're Happy Jack, namaste
y'all.

Namaste y'all, Happy Jack, namaste y'all."

Jack sang, danced and clapped to the beat of the genie's rap song. Ivanhoe and Petucan also sang, danced and clapped in circles around the happy genie.

Jack began to shine so brightly with all the love and kindness he felt living inside of him. It was the same light we all have that becomes brighter with good thoughts, good deeds and most of all with love.

With gratitude and joy, the genie happily whooshed back into the little rusty oil lamp as he and the lamp disappeared, leaving a sky-blue-pink misty trail behind.

Jack was happy. Jack was Happy Jack.

⋙ CHAPTER 7 ⋙

JACK-IN-THE-BOOK

"**I** want to stay here forever," announced a very happy Jack. "I don't ever want to wake up," he continued.

"You still haven't found Satya yet, the dreamer of all dreams," reminded Petucan.

"This isn't such a bad dream. There are no bullies here, and I don't have to run anymore," answered Jack.

With these words, the sky darkened. Ominous clouds started rolling in. Big drops of water pelted at them. Being stuffed with cotton, Petucan and Ivanhoe started to sag. Jack decided he did have to run after all.

"Quick, over there," he pointed as he ran.

They shivered under the eaves of the village bandstand, waiting for the rain to stop. The clouds swallowed the warmth of the sun and grumbled by mocking them as they stood in the gloom.

"Now what?" asked Jack. "Why'd it have to rain?"

"Nothing stays the same," answered Petucan. "Nature is the proof of that. It's always changing. Look at you, Jack. You're always growing, aren't you?"

"You don't change. You and Ivanhoe can't grow. You're both stuffed with cotton," he bounced back as his mood began to match the gloom.

"Ivanhoe has changed. He's lost an eye and his ear is falling off. And I wasn't always a monkey," replied Petucan.

"What were you before you were a monkey?" asked Jack.

With a smile, Petucan answered, "First I was a thought. Then I became words in a book. Now, I'm part of a story in a dream or maybe I'm a dream in a story. But to you, I'm a stuffed monkey and now I'm your friend. We all have lots of labels. But the secret is, we can be anything we want to be. You can be alone, Jack, but you don't have to be lonely."

And in his deep voice, Ivanhoe sang, "You're on the mend when you have a friend. If there's no one else, you still have your Self."

"Ivanhoe is right, Jack. You have to be a best friend to yourself. If you hate yourself then everyone else will see that and they won't like you either. You have to be your own best friend. You can rely on yourself, Jack. You can trust yourself. That's the secret. When you blame everyone else for your bad luck, it takes away your power to help yourself."

The sky began to lighten. As the sun once again warmed the day, the three of them set off towards the bright blue water they could see glinting a short way ahead. Jack hadn't realized they were so near the coast. They got to the shore in no time at all. It was just like living in a dream, which indeed Jack was.

As they walked along the beach, which was made up of small crushed shells that crunched under Jack's slippers, they saw a small figure sitting on a rock that jutted out towards the sea. As they neared the rock, they saw it was a small boy with tears in his eyes. The happiness left Jack as sadness crept over him. He was once again reminded that he was Happy Jack, the unhappiest boy in the world. Perhaps this boy was also escaping into a dream because he had no parents and was also bullied. But then, how had someone else gotten into Jack's dream?

"I'm Jack. What's your name?" he asked the boy who seemed a little older than him by a year or two even though he was so small. The boy looked like he should be singing Christmas carols at someone's front door. He certainly looked out of place sitting on a rock by the sea. Next to the boy lay a candle-lit lamp.

The little olive-skinned, brown-eyed, round-mouthed face was snuggled under a wool hat, which matched the striped wool scarf draping around his neck. He wore a knitted red sweater and dark green pants. The small boy's hands displayed knitted white mittens that clutched onto a large leather-bound book titled Classic Christmas Carols in gold letters gracing the front cover. However, on closer inspection, Jack saw the boy had no shoes and only one red sock.

"I'm the boy on the rock with the missing sock," said the boy on the rock with a missing sock. "My name's Ahimsa, and I'm not going to sing Christmas carols for you, so don't ask."

"Oh, um, okay. What're you doing here and why're you crying?' asked Jack a little perplexed.

"I was thrown away because my sock's missing," replied Ahimsa, "and I lost my shoes."

That hurt Jack to the quick. He knew exactly how the boy felt. "I was thrown away too," stated Jack. "When I think about it, I always end up crying as well."

"Don't jump to conclusions," scolded Ahimsa as he wiped away a stray tear. "I'm happy I was thrown away. I love it here. I kicked off my shoes and lost my sock on purpose. I knew if I did, I'd get thrown out. People don't like to keep things that are incomplete."

"But why? Why would you want to be thrown out and all alone?" asked Jack.

"I was sold as a Christmas ornament to a lady at the mall," he explained. "I was made to sing carols all through the Christmas holidays. I'm so over the Christmas thing because that was the only time I saw daylight. I was stuffed into a box for the rest of the year. Stuffed away and forgotten for a whole year. Imagine that! Even the elves and angels in the box with me were frustrated and angry. People celebrate you once a year and then they forget about you. It's like you're a story in a book and once the story has been read, the words disappear with the closing of the book until another year jogs their memory and they remember you existed. I only existed when people noticed me at Christmas, especially the kids. You'd think that was the only reason I existed. It's like I had no other purpose. They didn't even know my name. Who gets to decide my fate for me? I do have a free will you know," said Ahimsa continuing his rant.

"Oh," said Jack again, "then why're you crying?"

"Because I'm hungry," came the reply in harmony with a loud belly rumble.

"Oh," said Jack for the third time as he patted his pajama pocket instinctively knowing he had no food.

"We can fish for you," suggested Petucan, hopping around excitedly because he loved to fish.

"Wonderful! I love eating fish. I'm so done with turkey and stuffing and ugh, those horrible cranberries," said the boy on the rock with only one sock. "One year, I pushed the turkey off the table when no one was looking. They blamed the dog," he laughed.

Ivanhoe was not amused and sang so, "You are so naughty and your blame was faulty. You're out of your mind if you can't be kind."

"It was only a little fun," defended Ahimsa. "It took the edge off my job. Singing Christmas carols over and over again is so boring and sometimes, I even ended up with a sore throat. The lady who bought me perched me in the front window, and when she opened my book, I'd have to start singing when the music automatically started playing. I couldn't turn it off and she'd always forget. I'm solar-powered, so I can never run out of energy. It's very hot sitting in the front window all day, even when there's snow on the ground. People don't think about these things, especially when they are busy during Christmas. What's your names?" he asked Petucan and Ivanhoe without skipping a beat.

"This is Ivanhoe and I'm Petucan," answered Petucan.

"Can I pet you, Petucan?" asked Ahimsa with sparkles of laughter in his eyes.

"No, keep your hands to yourself. I'm a monkey, not a pet. Don't you dare pet me," replied Petucan as he petted Ivanhoe on the head.

"Okay, okay, keep your tail on," he replied taking a couple of steps back and grinning with his hands up in surrender.

"We don't have any fishing poles," said Jack trying to change the subject. As soon as the words were spoken, a fishing pole appeared in Petucan's hand.

"Let me guess. We're in Dhyāna Land, and we can dream what we want," said Jack as he also wondered why Ahimsa hadn't dreamt up food for himself.

"It's because it's your dream," said Petucan in answer to Jack's wondering mind. "You are the only dreamer in this story. And since I have the fishing pole, I guess I'm the only fishermonkey in this story."

As Petucan fished, Jack, Ivanhoe and Ahimsa built a firepit and started a dream fire. They ate fish and the scallops Ivanhoe had found in the tidepool nearby. It was all yummy and delicious.

Jack began to think about Christmas. He couldn't remember one single Christmas spent with his parents. He couldn't remember what toys his parents had given him.

"I don't believe in Santa," he announced, surprising everyone.

"Why not?" asked Ahimsa.

"He's make-believe. That's why," answered Jack.

"No, he's not," argued the boy.

"Yes, he is," claimed Jack. "You'll only find him in a story book. He's not real."

"I've met him. I was made in India and sent to the North Pole. I met him at the North Pole before I was shipped off to the mall. He said hello to me and said I had a lovely singing voice," countered Ahimsa.

"Well, I don't believe in Santa. That's for little kids."

"I'm not a little kid, and I've met him. He's real," said Ahimsa standing on his rock in his best red sock.

"You're not real," disputed Jack. "You're a Christmas ornament."

"I am real. If I wasn't real, I wouldn't get hungry. You're the one who's not real."

Petucan and Ivanhoe listened quietly to the squabbling boys.

"Am too!" said Jack.

"How do you know? How do you know you're a real boy? You might be a story in a book," Ahimsa challenged. "That's it! You're a Jack-in-the-Book and only pop out when the pages are opened," he scoffed.

Jack was silenced. How did he know? He knew he was in Dhyāna Land and this was a dream. But he was still a boy, whether he was dreaming or not. He was sure he was a boy. What else could he be? He wasn't a stuffed toy or an ornament.

He looked at Petucan. He looked at Ivanhoe. "Yes," he thought, they were definitely stuffed toys. But they were real toys even if they weren't human. He looked at Ahimsa. He saw the small round mouth ready to sing for the existence of Santa. Yes, he thought, Ahimsa was definitely a solar-powered toy ornament. "Toys are real, aren't they?" he asked himself. Then he made up his mind. If he was real, they weren't real. You're either alive or not. But they weren't dead either. If he touched them, he would be able to feel them. It was all so confusing.

"I'm the only one that's real," he said to them all as he wondered what made things not real.

"Real people don't live in stories and dreams," maintained Ahimsa.

"They can if they want to," argued Jack as he looked around him and then at Petucan for support. "And what's more, dreams are real dreams," he continued, repeating Petucan's words.

"Well, my book is real," affirmed Ahimsa as he hugged his book of Christmas carols like a sacred bible. "So, if Santa is written in there, which he IS, then he's real too! Santa exists just like ink on a page exists, so there!"

"Well, I've never seen him," argued Jack.

"And I've never seen a thought, but I can think!" Ahimsa shot back.

Jack felt the argument was going around in circles. And this particular circle was getting wound tighter and tighter. He took a deep breath and looked up at the stars just in time to see one shooting across the night sky. Like a shooting star, thoughts began to fly back and forth in his mind. He wondered why he felt real. He knew he was but how did he know? What was it that made him so sure? What was it he felt deep down inside of him? And then the answer came.

The answer lay in the question. He was real because he could ask himself that question. If he wasn't real, he couldn't ask himself if he was real or not. He wouldn't even be able to think about it if it wasn't true. That's what made him real, he thought. There was more to him than just his reflection in a mirror. There was something beneath his skin. Something that could listen to his thoughts. Something that was more.

He thought of the fish they had caught. "Can a fish ask themselves if they are real or not?" he pondered.

Were they real because he had eaten one? He wondered what had become of the fish he had eaten. Was the fish now a part of him or was he what he ate? Was he a part of a fish? It was all so perplexing. Just like a mysterious dream in a children's book.

Ahimsa smiled at the confused boy. He knew he had fed Jack impossible questions and because of it, he knew Jack would remain hungry. Ahimsa understood that this was his real purpose, the reason why he existed: To keep Jack hungry for answers. He never intended to cause Jack any hurt. Quite the opposite. He wanted to make Jack feel real—more real than he had ever felt in his whole life. That was the gift Ahimsa wanted to give to Jack, even if it wasn't yet Christmas in Dhyāna Land. He knew it was the best gift Jack would ever receive: the gift of wonder, the gift of curiosity.

Ahimsa was happy. His job was done. He yawned a loud satisfying yawn making sure everyone heard because that was another thing he knew. He knew yawns were catching.

One after another, they all began to yawn. Tiredness enveloped them as darkness cloaked the remnants of the day. The moon danced on the waves as stars twinkled in the warm night sky.

"Wake up! Come on Jack, wake up!" said a soft voice.

As he tossed and turned, his strawberry blond head began to rise from the soft lumpy fur on Ivanhoe's back.

"Jack, wake up! You're having another bad dream," urged the gentle voice.

Jack sat bolt upright, feeling the shells crunch and shift beneath him. He was dreaming but knew it wasn't the nightmare he was used to having because in this dream, he wasn't being chased. He had dreamt that he was doing the chasing. He had dreamt he was chasing fish that outswam him. He told his dream out loud since this was the first dream he had ever remembered.

"Why do you think you were chasing fish in a dream?" asked Petucan.

When Jack thought about it, he realized that when they went on their way in the morning, the small boy would become hungry again because there would be no one to fish for him.

"You can teach me to fish," said Ahimsa wiping sleep from his eyes. "There is never a bad time to go fishing. Once I know how to fish, I'll never ever be hungry because I can rely on myself for food," he added. "Since I enjoyed visiting the North Pole and meeting Santa, you can leave me the fishing pole, so I'll always be near the pole," he continued as he laughed at his own joke.

Jack smiled. As challenging as he was, he liked the willful boy on the rock. Indeed, Ahimsa even slept on the rock with his book and one sock. He could hear the boy suggesting to himself which fish were naughty and which were nice. "Something he has probably picked up from Santa or the elves," he thought, forgetting he didn't believe in Santa. He heard the boy conclude that all the fish were nice because they never tasted salty. They always remained fresh even though they lived in a salty sea. "Perhaps we can all learn a thing or two from a fish," mused Jack as the sounds of the whispering surf tucked him in.

Petucan loved to fish so much, he decided he would stay up and show Ahimsa how to fish from his rock. The boy was excited to learn. He was very attentive and caught a few fish, which he immediately released back into the sea as he was still full from dinner. It wasn't until the early hours that he and Petucan bedded down and started to softly snore in harmony with the waves caressing the shore.

Abruptly, they all woke up to a loud whistle and stood agape as a train came to a screeching halt just behind a row of palm trees lining the shore.

❧❧ CHAPTER 8 ❧❧

THE MINDLESS EXPRESS

"All aboard!" cried the conductor. "The next stop is Quiet Place Station. All aboard, hurry along now."

Jack, Petucan and Ivanhoe looked at one another then at the boy on the rock.

"What are you waiting for? Christmas?" asked Ahimsa, once again laughing at his own joke. "Thanks to you, I'm self-sufficient," he added seriously.

Jack, Petucan and Ivanhoe did not need to be told twice. They said their goodbyes to the boy and left him sitting on his rock with his bright red sock, fishing pole in hand, singing Christmas carols where he began using naughty words in place of the original words. They decided it was best to leave quickly as the words became more embarrassingly naughty.

All three climbed up the four steps that led onto the back of the end train car, opened the door and entered.

"Wow," said Jack. "Look at all that food. We must be in the dining car."

It was then that Jack's stomach let out a loud growl. He was hungry and it was time for breakfast. Ivanhoe whimpered and began to drool when he spotted the stitched wool biscuits in a dog bowl. Even Petucan hungered for the jar of cotton wool balls sitting at the end of the table.

"Sit down, sit down," said the conductor when he entered the dining car. "Tickets first then you can eat."

As soon as they sat down, Jack realized he didn't have a ticket. Then he realized the train had started inching forward away from the shore as the boy on the rock, complete with one sock, disappeared from view.

"You'll have to stop the train," he said to the conductor. "We don't have a ticket. We didn't see a ticket booth and we don't have any money. Sorry," he apologized getting redder in the face. It was a good job no one else was in the dining car to see his embarrassment.

"Of course, you have a ticket," the conductor replied. "Everyone has a ticket to wherever they want to go."

"But..."

"Come on now, show me your ticket."

"It's okay, Jack. We have our tickets," Petucan butted in. "Sorry," he said to the conductor, "it's his first time on the Mindless Express."

Jack was confused. He knew he hadn't bought a ticket.

Petucan explained, "Everyone has a ticket to wherever they want to go. All they have to do is know where they are going. If you don't know where you're going, you can't go where you want. That's the ticket."

"Okaaay?" responded Jack.

"So, what's your destination?" asked the conductor.

"It's the quiet place," answered Jack as he thought of his quest to find Satya.

As soon as they all thought of the quiet place, three tickets appeared on the table in front of them. Jack picked up his ticket and saw it was blank. He looked at the conductor confused.

"Have you been there before?" asked the conductor.

"No," answered Jack.

"Then it might take a little longer to get there," said the conductor.

"How long?"

"A few days. Maybe even a few weeks," advised the conductor.

As he punched a hole in each ticket, the conductor shared the fact that a young girl once spent a fortnight on the train before it came to a stop.

"What's a fortnight?" asked Jack.

"Two weeks; you know, fourteen nights," responded Petucan.

"Wow. That's a long time to be sitting on a train. What did she find to do in a fortnight?" quizzed Jack.

"She found plenty to do to kill time. Eat up and enjoy the ride," smiled the conductor at an astonished Jack.

Jack looked at the conductor's back disappearing into the car ahead. He looked at Petucan with questions in his eyes.

"Let's eat, I'm hungry," said Petucan in answer to his unspoken questions.

Jack filled his plate with eggs, hash browns, fried chicken, shrimp and raisin toast with a Reese's Peanut Butter Cup on the side.

"What?" asked Jack when he saw Petucan looking at his plate. "They're my favorites. Who decided what should go with what on a plate anyway?" he continued in defense.

"You do have a point, Jack. I was just thinking how unhealthy it looks. If you don't look after your body; your mind and even your feelings will come to resemble the jumble on your plate," advised Petucan.

"Well it looks healthy to me, so mind your own breakfast," said Jack, rolling his eyes.

"Would you like some strawberry juice to wash it all down?" Petucan asked as he set down a large bowl of multi-colored cotton wool balls on the table opposite Jack.

"Yes please. Is that what you like to eat?" asked Jack, pointing at the fluffy balls.

"Yes. I like regular food, but this is my favorite. After a bowl this big, I always feel nice and stuffed," he giggled as he got up to get their drinks and a bowl of cold water for Ivanhoe. Ivanhoe was already digging into his wooly dog biscuits.

"Wow, that was great," said Jack as he looked out of the window, out to the passing meadows and trees. Out to the fields of yellow and red flowers. Out to the passing lakes full of swans. Feeling sated, he sighed with contentment as the scenery passed by. "I could stay on this train forever," he confessed as he melted into the velvet seat.

"You may have to if you don't know where you're going," advised Petucan. "If you can't picture the quiet place in your mind, then we'll all go travelling mindlessly along in Dhyāna Land. We'll never get anywhere."

"How can I picture the quiet place when I've never been there? I've never seen it. How can I possibly know how to get there?" he asked turning back to Petucan as if he had all the answers.

"You have the answers within you," said Petucan.

Ivanhoe had finished his bowl of biscuits and was listening to the conversation. He jumped on the seat to sit beside Jack. As Jack put his arms around him,

83

Ivanhoe sung in his deep voice, "The Mindless Express is just a test. To see if you know where you want to go. You can go far, you can stay near. You need an idea for things to appear."

"What d'ya mean by that, Ivanhoe?" asked Jack. "What're you telling me?"

Ivanhoe continued, "It's a slow steady pace to find the quiet place. You have to mention a clear intention. Your fears bring tears, but you'll flourish with courage. Don't be afraid and don't be swayed. Don't sit on the side; you'll get taken for a ride. Decide what you need and take the lead. You'll arrive at the station your true destination. And there you will find some peace of mind."

"I need to find the quiet place," said Jack in frustration. "Stop singing in riddles Ivanhoe."

"You're simply confused and at a loss. Always know, you are your boss. There is nothing to fear, the quiet place is near. Now start to believe or take your leave. If you don't believe, you'll never go far. You'll never go far from this Mindless Train car," finished Ivanhoe in his deep voice.

Exasperated, Jack got up and sidled past Ivanhoe, heading for the front end of the train. He opened the door and stepped onto the next platform between the cars. Opening the door to the next car, he found to his delight a whole wall of game machines. There were video games, a virtual reality game, and a basketball shooting game. There were games to collect points and games to lose points. Games of skill and games to kill. There were pinball machines and arcade machines. Happiness filled Jack as he headed to the nearest game.

Engrossed in so much fun, Jack hadn't noticed Petucan and Ivanhoe coming into the game car. He bounced from playing virtual video games to shooting plastic ducks to racing cars on a 3-D screen.

Petucan and Ivanhoe sat and watched Jack having fun. There were so many machines, he spun around playing for hours. The train mindlessly chugged along the tracks as Jack mindlessly played game-after-game. He was so engrossed, he hadn't noticed the sun's journey across the darkening sky.

"Jack," said Petucan gently, "it's getting late."

Coming out of his gaming stupor, Jack turned to the window and saw the darkness skulking outside, but it wasn't the darkness that shocked him. It was the barren landscape. There were no trees, no fields, no lakes and no flowers. There was nothing. The horizon had disappeared. Jack couldn't tell where the land met the sky. Everything seemed to melt into nothingness. The dark grey yawned, ready to swallow him out of existence.

"Petucan, what's happened? Why's there nothing out there?" he panicked.

"You're on the Mindless Express," replied Petucan. "When your mind is distracted with all these game machines, you become mindless. When you don't think, your mind becomes blank. You don't use your imagination anymore. You don't plan and you stop looking forward. Television can do the same thing if you're not careful. It can stop you from using your mind. When you stop using your mind, you chug along on the Mindless Express going nowhere. You forget to look at how beautiful the world is. Your energy flows where your attention goes and then drains away until nothing is left. The more you play with machines, the less you play in the world around you. Eventually, your world disappears because you've forgotten about it. You wake up one day and find it all gone. It's too late. You've wasted your time on the Mindless Express. You lose your chance to make a difference in the world. Your story never gets told."

Jack was not liking the emptiness outside the window. It gave him a headache trying to make something out of nothing. He felt as hollow as the void outside. It was as if he were being stripped of all purpose and becoming unreal.

"Let's get some rest, Jack," advised Petucan. "Perhaps things will look different in the morning."

Aimlessly, Jack got up and followed Petucan to the front of the game car. When they entered the next train car, there were two large compartments, each with a basin to wash, a bed and fresh nightshirts folded neatly on the stool next to their beds. There was also a nice clean toothbrush with red-mint toothpaste. Jack decided he needed to wash thoroughly and scrub away the bad thoughts beginning to build in his mind. And, he definitely needed to clean his teeth to get rid of the sour taste in his mouth.

Each compartment had curtains for privacy. Jack knew which compartment he wanted to take because there was a large soft cushion in one of them for Ivanhoe. Petucan smiled as he wished Jack and Ivanhoe goodnight.

"Wake up! Come on, Jack, wake up!" said the soft voice.

As he tossed and turned, his strawberry blond head sank deeper into his pillow.

"Jack, wake up! You're having another bad dream," urged the gentle voice.

Sitting bolt upright in his bed, Jack could feel his face covered with sweat as he stared at the soft glow by his bed.

"Jack. Come on, wake up. It's only another dream," said Petucan.

"My nightmare's back. I hate bedtime. I hate my bad dreams," cried Jack.

After all this time, he felt safe crying in front of Petucan because he instinctively knew Petucan wouldn't see him as being weak. He trusted the monkey completely and felt he could tell him all his worries, and he did just that. He got everything off his chest and felt better for it.

"It won't be long before the sun rises. Why don't we get washed and dressed, then we can have a nice breakfast?" soothed Petucan.

"Where do you think we are now?" asked Jack as he eyed his neatly folded pajamas wondering how they were freshly washed and ironed.

"We're on a train," teased Petucan, hoping to lighten Jack's spirit.

"Funny. I know that," said Jack a little irritated as he snapped the curtains together to shut Petucan out.

He wasn't in the mood for jokes, especially after his experience of yesterday. He was scared of disappearing like the outside world had when he'd gotten so involved with games. That was probably the reason his nightmare had once again stalked him in his sleep.

When they were ready, Jack took the lead walking to the back end of the car and opened the door. With a gasp, he immediately jumped back, slamming the door with fright. He'd stopped himself just in time from falling off the back of the moving train. The train cars they had been in the day before had disappeared. It made no sense.

"What's happened to the train cars?" gasped Jack. "The game car and the dining car aren't hitched to the back of the train. I didn't know we'd stopped during the night."

"We didn't," said Petucan.

"Then where's the cars?" he asked as he looked out of the window, relieved to see meadows and trees.

Ivanhoe moved to Jack's side and sang, "It's a fact you can never go back. We all move ahead even when we're misled."

"We have to keep moving forward, Jack. There's no going back." said Petucan. "Come on, let's get breakfast."

Petucan moved to the front end of the sleeping car, opened the door and stepped into the dining car with Jack and Ivanhoe in tow. It was the exact same dining car from yesterday.

"I don't get it," said Jack. "How come the dining car is now in front instead of behind?"

"You remembered it from yesterday, so it still exists in the pages of your memory. It exists because you're hungry and you want to eat," answered Petucan. "Only now, the dining car is in front because it's in your future."

With his head full of thoughts and his plate full of food, Jack sat down and began digging into cherry pie, chocolate pancakes and pecan waffles topped with cream. Then he washed it all down with a glass of ice-cold strawberry milk. When he had finished, he sat back in his seat looking at the door in the front of the dining car, wondering what he would find if he opened it. Confused, he was beginning to feel as if he were traveling nowhere. He desperately wanted the train to stop so he could get off. With that thought came a loud whistle. The train slowed with a squealing of breaks until it finally came to a halt at the next station.

"Is this Quiet Place Station?" asked Jack knowing he still couldn't picture it in his mind.

"Only one way to find out," answered Petucan as he got up.

Jack and Ivanhoe followed. They stepped into a warm sunny day with a backdrop of mountains covered with snow at their peaks. Jack could hear birds tweeting in the trees and cows mooing in the meadow.

"Well, I guess it's not the quiet place if I can hear sounds," he observed.

"And I'm guessing you're right," responded Petucan. "We must have missed our stop when the outside disappeared. Let's go and explore," he continued as he turned toward the direction of the trees that lined the meadow.

As Jack turned around, the Mindless Express had gone. He was not surprised that the train had vanished without a sound. It seemed to make sense in Dhyāna Land. He fell in alongside Petucan as Ivanhoe sniffed his way a few steps ahead.

❧ CHAPTER 9 ❧

A LESSON IN THE WOODS

"It's this way," argued Jack. "No, it isn't. We've already been that way," argued Petucan.

They had been walking in circles for what seemed like hours. They had been arguing for what seemed like days. Everything looked the same. As Jack looked up to the dizzying high trees, the sun looked down at the dizzy confused boy.

Dizzy, because Jack found himself suddenly alone. Petucan and Ivanhoe had disappeared. He called out to them and nothing came back. He searched this way and that way, and that way became this way. Jack was hopelessly lost. He continued to look for his friends calling their names.

"Hoo-hoo, hoo-hoo, boo-hoo-hoo," Jack heard as he walked through the dense woods. His ears followed the sound and soon, he found himself standing in a little glade edged with daffodils. He saw a spotted owl sitting on a low branch. The owl was very tiny for a wood owl and wore silky brown feathers, flecked with whitish-grey cross-shaped markings. The flecks were as big as the owl's red-rimmed eyes, which widened upon seeing Jack.

"What's the matter?" asked Jack.

"Boo-hoo-hoo. Boo-hoo, who are you?" asked the owl in answer.

"I'm Jack. Why're you crying?"

"I'm not crying; I'm hooing," said the owl defensively.

"Well, it sure sounded like crying to me," responded Jack.

"Hooing is not the same as crying. And my name is Mac," he shot right back.

"Happy Mac, Happy Mac, run little fowl. Happy Mac, Happy Mac, we're on the prowl," Jack heard coming towards them.

The taunting song reminded Jack of the bullies who always chased him to and from school. Jack wondered if he'd have to rescue the little owl but the owl stayed perched on the low branch standing its ground, or rather its tree, as a fox, a rabbit and a skunk came into the clearing.

"What's the matter, Happy Mac? Are you hooting or are you tooting?" they jeered.

"Leave him alone," demanded Jack.

"What's it to you? Mind your own business," they said in unison.

"You shouldn't pick on people," stated Jack.

"You're a smart one, aren't you? He's an owl, not a person," said the smug skunk facing away from Jack with its tail up.

"Stop right there," came a deep voice at the edge of the clearing before the skunk could unleash its nasty spray.

The fox, rabbit and skunk quickly disappeared as Jack, turning toward the voice, came face-to-nose with a very regal stag. The tall red stag was crowned with velvet antlers that were about half its body size.

Indeed, the antlers were so large they looked like eight giant limbs of an old oak tree. The stag trotted daintily into the clearing until it stood rack and shoulders above Jack.

"Hello, I'm AlberJohn Berry," said the stag bowing low, "and you are?"

"Jack," said Jack as he stood agape.

"Thank you, Jack, for helping Mac," thanked the stag as he trotted toward the low branch where the owl perched.

The owl stretched out its talons and latched onto the stag's antler. The stag turned with the owl perched on top of his antler and headed back in the direction it had come from.

"It's a pleasure to meet you, Jack. Indeed, a pleasure to be sure," continued the stag as it passed.

"Wait! Have you seen a monkey and a dog?" asked Jack. "I've lost my friends. We got split up."

"Ah, yes. I believe I have. I passed them on my way here. Follow me," invited the stag as it left the clearing.

Jack had a hard time keeping up. His feet were not as dainty as the stag's. He couldn't help but slide on the damp leaves and he would often trip over roots and small stones. The stag slowed so Jack could catch up. As they walked on, the woods thinned, giving way to a clearing full of bluebells. The bluebells tinkled as they passed as if enjoying a small joke that Jack didn't quite get.

"It's not far now, my dear boy," said the stag.

There was a thicket ahead where Jack saw a trail winding through the forest inviting them to come in. They followed the trail and came upon a beautiful young deer with golden eyes peeking out from very long eyelashes.

"If you don't mind, this is my hind," introduced the stag. "Her name is Lady Felicity."

"She's a very beautiful lady," said Jack before he could stop himself. "Er, sorry," he continued as his face reddened.

"Please, you don't have to apologize when you tell the truth," responded AlberJohn Berry. "And, you've met Mac, of course. This is Buck," he continued, "although he's not a buck; he's a duck."

Jack looked to where AlberJohn Berry had nodded. There, a duckling sat on top of a small nest preening itself. It was the ugliest duckling Jack had ever seen. However, he wasn't going to state the truth this time. That would be mean.

"It's okay, my dear boy. The duck knows how handsome he is," said AlberJohn Berry reading his thoughts.

"I'm going to be a swan," said the duckling as it stopped preening to look up at Jack.

Jack had seen a cygnet before. This was definitely a duck.

Lady Felicity smiled. "I hear you're looking for your friends," she said. "They are hunting for mushrooms and blackberries. They won't be long. Why don't you make yourself at home?" she invited.

Very shortly, Petucan and Ivanhoe could be heard singing a happy song as they headed back to where Jack sat.

"There you are," said Petucan. "We thought we'd lost you. We bumped into AlberJohn Berry and Lady Felicity, and they said they could hear you talking to Mac. They're very sensitive that way. They hear everything that goes on in these woods. AlberJohn Berry offered to find you and bring you back. Are you hungry?" he asked displaying hands loaded with mushrooms and berries.

"Make yourselves comfortable," said Lady Felicity. "Ah, here is Hedgewick," she continued as a hedgehog came into view. "Now you've met my whole family."

"Family?" questioned Jack. "I thought a deer had fawns," he stated thinking of an old movie he had seen on television. "You have an owl, a duck and a hedgehog. That doesn't make sense."

"When something doesn't make sense, it's simply because you don't have a full understanding. You don't know the whole story. It's like reading the beginning of a book and then the end without knowing what happened in the middle," offered AlberJohn Berry.

"Oh, I see," said Jack thoughtfully.

"Do you, Jack?" asked AlberJohn Berry.

"Well no. I guess I don't. I don't know why you have an owl, a duck and a hedgehog instead of fawns," replied Jack. "Perhaps you took them in to save them or something. You're right, I don't really know the full story."

"Their moms and dads abandoned them so we adopted them," said Lady Felicity full of love.

Jack didn't like this story. It was his story except he hadn't been adopted. "What horrible parents they must've had. They're lucky to be rid of them," he thought aloud.

"Now, now Jack. Don't be angry. We don't know the reasons why they were abandoned. Perhaps their parents were sick. Perhaps they didn't get along with each other. Perhaps they thought it would be best for their offspring to find a better home. No matter the reason, it happened and the only thing we can do is make the best of it," advised Lady Felicity.

"But it's not fair. The owl was crying and being bullied. I saw it. That's what happens when you're thrown away. That's what happens when no one wants you," said Jack becoming more annoyed.

AlberJohn Berry and Lady Felicity looked at Jack, waiting for him to calm, as Petucan and Ivanhoe sat and listened, eager to learn from the mindful stag and hind.

"Life by its very nature is a challenge. It's just like going to school. You learn and then you're tested. If you don't understand what you've learnt, you must retake the test, maybe over and over again until you begin to understand. It's called life's lessons in a school of rainy days and bright sunshine. The more you learn and become aware, the easier it is for you to forecast what lies ahead. It's called intuition," instructed Lady Felicity.

AlberJohn Berry continued Jack's education, "There are predators in these woods. There are sly foxes, mean skunks and rabbits that will skip out on you when you need them the most. The only way to be safe is to learn who you are; then, you can become who you want to be. You can learn to be strong, and learn to save yourself. We adopt lots of animals, so they can learn to stand on their own feet, or paws, or hooves," said AlberJohn Berry, "but we never forget; a fox will always be a sly fox. A skunk will continue to be a smelly skunk, and a rabbit will continue to hop. Even a hedgehog will prick you if you get too close. Everyone lives up to their true nature but you're different, Jack. You can think. You can think about what it is you want to be, and then you can become how you think. You have a choice, Jack."

Lady Felicity continued where AlberJohn Berry left off, "You can blame your difficulties on your parents, but every time you do, it's like sitting in mud. Each time you blame, you sink a little further until you get stuck. When you get stuck, you can't act to make things better. You won't become anything if you keep blaming. You'll always be stuck in the mud. But when you stop blaming, then you can act. You can act like people do in fairy tales. You can write your own lines. You can create your own story. What do you want your story to be, Jack?"

This made Jack think. He thought about it a lot. It was the smell of frying mushrooms and soft-boiled blackberries smothered in honey that broke into Jack's thoughts as Petucan placed a large leaf of food on his lap.

"Eat up, Jack," said Petucan, "before it gets cold."

Jack chewed on mushrooms and berries as he chewed over what he had just heard. Ivanhoe left to scavenge for his own food. He soon returned licking his lips. He lay down by Jack's side and in his deep voice, he sang, "Oh deer, oh deer, what wonderful deer. Their hearts are kind. The stag and the hind."

"Thank you, Ivanhoe," said Lady Felicity. "Why don't you all get some sleep? A nice rest will do you good."

"Goodnight," hooted Mac.

"Goodnight," quacked Buck.

"Goodnight," huffed Hedgewick.

"Goodnight everyone. Sweet dreams," said AlberJohn Berry and Lady Felicity.

But dreams are not always sweet.

CHAPTER 10

THE LYING MOUNTAIN

They got up the next morning and after a breakfast of more mushrooms and blackberries smothered in honey, they said goodbye and headed towards the snowcapped mountains.

It took half a day to reach the base of the nearest mountain. The climb was easy and all three kept a steady pace. The air began to cool the more they climbed. The wildflowers and shrubs thinned until there was nothing but giant boulders with a path of loose gravel running between them. It was late in the afternoon when they came to the mouth of a cave.

"I'm tired," said Jack. "Can we rest for a while?"

"Why don't we rest here for the night?" suggested Petucan as Ivanhoe wagged his tail in agreement.

"That's a great idea," said Jack relieved at not having to walk anymore, "and it's not too cold. It'll be fun to camp here, and we have a cave in case it rains," he continued as he put down the grass-weaved bag of apples, mushrooms and berries they had picked while traveling through the woods.

They sat down and ate supper as they watched the darkness approach. It wasn't long before tiny lights pin-pricked the night sky as the stars winked on. A halo appeared on the horizon and the moon began to rise. Awed by the enormous globe of light, they sat and stared. The moon took on a life of its own as it stared right back.

They could hear the night whispering to them, enticing them, urging them to come closer. Jack was falling into the moon. He shook his head. He felt he was going to disappear into the rising stillness. He turned to Petucan who was looking in the opposite direction. He was looking deep into the cave as if he were trying to see what would be revealed. Ivanhoe got to his feet with a low rumble in his throat.

"What is it, Petucan? What's that sound? What are those little lights down there?" asked Jack as he pointed to where Petucan gazed.

"They're mountain lyings," answered Petucan.

"Mountain lions?" Jack repeated afraid.

"No. They're mountain lyings," said Petucan. "They're harmless but not to be believed. They live in caves on Lying Mountain. This is the Lying Mountain. There must be water in there since they are living here. They always live around water. Let's go inside. They won't hurt you."

Jack was skeptical and wanted to stay outside with Ivanhoe. He was also thirsty, plus he didn't want Petucan to go into the cave on his own. He was worried in case Petucan would get lost and he and Ivanhoe would be left sitting on the side of Lying Mountain. He'd gotten used to having Petucan around and he wasn't sure how he would awake from this dream without him. The dream could take him anywhere. It could take him to a place where he didn't want to go.

"Really, it's quite safe, Jack. I've met them before. Come on, let's go in," said Petucan reading Jack's expression.

Petucan began putting the leftover mushrooms and berries into the bag and stood up. Jack and Ivanhoe reluctantly followed him deeper into the cave.

They didn't have to go too far into the cave before they came upon a small pool of water. The water, still as a glass mirror, was lit up by orange mountain lyings flying above. The mountain lyings resembled tiny furry bats with a small round ball of light at the end of their nose that shone bright. There may have been fifty of them silently flying around. They were busy little things, so it was hard to count. As Jack followed the little orange furry things flying to and fro, he was amused when the mountain lyings gave off a little sneeze. The small bright light shot off their nose winking out as soon as the light touched the water. Almost instantaneously, a new light grew back on the end of their nose.

Jack was amazed and not afraid at all. He thought they were cute in a batty kind of way. He sat on a large bolder at the edge of the pool and held up his hand to see if one would land on his outstretched palm. One mountain lying decided to rest on his finger hanging upside down just like a bat. Another hung on the end of Ivanhoe's tail, which caused Ivanhoe to run in circles trying to catch it. Petucan laughed as he sat next to Jack.

The night wore on as eyelids began to lower. Mesmerized by the winking mountain lyings, they began to yawn. It wasn't too far to slide silently from the boulder to the floor and Jack did just that. The floor was even and smooth. Soon, soft snores harmonized playfully with the winking lights cast by the mountain lyings.

"Your mom didn't want you. Your dad didn't want you. Nobody wants you. All the other kids think you're weak. You're a scaredy cat. Run, Jack, run."

Jack began to toss and turn his strawberry blond head.

"Happy Jack, Happy Jack, run far away. Happy Jack, Happy Jack, don't you come back."

Jack began to whimper in his sleep.

"Nobody wants you. Run away and never come back."

Jack began crying.

"Sad Sack Jack. Sad Sack Jack."

A loud cry escaped Jack's lips.

"Wake up! Come on, Jack, wake up!" said the soft voice. "You're having another bad dream."

As he sat up, Jack could feel his face covered with sweat.

"Jack. Come on, wake up. It's only another dream."

He shook himself awake and looked around. Then he looked directly into Petucan's questioning eyes.

"They were chasing me. They were calling me names," cried Jack. "No one wants me. They hate me. No one loves me. They threw me away. No one's ever loved me," Jack sobbed as Petucan put his arm around Jack's shaking shoulders. "Leave me alone. Don't touch me. I don't need you. I don't need anyone. Just leave me alone," demanded Jack as he shoved Petucan away. Ivanhoe crouched low to the ground afraid that Jack would push him away too. Jack continued to sob.

"Jack..."

"Don't talk to me. I thought I was safe with you. Safe with you and Ivanhoe. But you're just a useless monkey," accused Jack.

"Jack..."

"I said don't talk to me. Go away."

Jack continued to sob. He sobbed even when his tears had finally dried out. There were no more tears to be had. He could only feel the hurt, as if love had no place in his heart. Petucan had lied to him. Love didn't exist. There was only hurt and tears to be found.

As his sobbing ebbed, Jack took a deep ragged breath. He felt the cool air enter his lungs. Felt the hard floor beneath him. Felt his pajamas against his skin and the slippers on his feet. He could even feel the hair on his head and sense the freckles on his face. He took another deep breath as he looked around. He saw the mountain lyings and felt their soft breeze as they continued flying to and fro. The bright lights still winked out as they landed on the water when the mountain lyings sneezed. For the first time, Jack noticed that some of the lights were brighter than others. They started out having the same brightness; however, some of the lights got very bright, some stayed the same, and some even dimmed a little. Jack's senses sharpened as if he were discovering new sounds, sights, textures and smells. When he spoke, it was as if he had never heard his own voice before. Even his voice seemed to have a new flavor. Everything seemed brighter in the soft darkness.

"It's good to cry, Jack. It's good to get it out and then let it go. Crying creates space inside of you so you can be open to new things. Crying helps you let go," said Petucan.

"I'm sorry, Petucan. I didn't mean to shout at you and push you away. I was scared."

"Jack, thank you for saying sorry. I know you didn't mean it and know you were scared. You should always honor how you feel. You shouldn't run away from your feelings because feelings are real. Feelings are something you experience. You feel the way you do for a reason. You should never hide behind feelings or try and stuff them away somewhere. Feelings exist just like thoughts exist," said Petucan.

"But I shouldn't take it out on you or Ivanhoe... ever. You're my friends. I love you both."

As soon as the word love appeared in the air between them, the mountain lyings flew up to the roof of the cave and hung upside down with their wings folded. Their noses began to dim as a warm humming embraced the cool night. Jack looked at Petucan for an answer to his unspoken question.

"They're snoring. They have to rest sometime," explained Petucan. "They're sleeping. I think the word love made them tired. The truth always relaxes them.

And just so you know, they are the reason you had your nightmare," he went on. "They are mountain lyings and they like to live up to their name. Sorry, I should have warned you."

"They made me have my nightmare?" questioned Jack.

"Yes. They gathered all the lies you believe in and played with them in your head."

"How do they know what I believe in?" asked Jack.

"They know all the lies in the world. They like to collect lies and play with them. When they have finished playing with a lie, they sneeze the lie off the end of their nose so the lie lands in the pool of water and disappears forever," answered Petucan.

"You mean all those little lights at the end of their noses are lies?"

"Yes," came the simple reply.

"Why are some brighter than others?"

"Some are little lies. Adults call them white lies. Some are childish lies that are told when a child wants to get out of trouble. Some are bad lies that are told to get people into trouble or when someone doesn't feel good about themselves. Some people tell lies to make themselves look better or to get what they want. Some are very bad lies when people are being mean," explained Petucan. "There are many lies of all shapes and sizes. No one can hide behind a lie, especially the big ones. The bigger they are, the heavier they get until a person is weighed down so much, they can't get up again," he continued.

"But a lie is still a lie," said Jack.

"Yes, it is, but some people experience lies as the truth," Petucan responded.

"How can a lie be the truth?" asked Jack. "That doesn't make sense."

"It can't be the truth. You just think it is. It's called lying to yourself. You might believe something to be the truth when in fact it's not true at all."

"What d'ya mean, Petucan?" asked a confused Jack.

"When you were crying, you said that no one loves you, but that's not true. I love you and Ivanhoe also loves you," answered Petucan feeling it was safe to say that without Jack getting mad or sad. "The mountain lyings knew you were lying to yourself even if you didn't know it. They were frolicking with all the lies you tell yourself and all the lies you believe in. They were playing with all the lies you learnt from the bullies chasing you, telling you that you were a scaredy cat. That's why you had your nightmare. They were making you remember lies. The mountain lyings really do live up to their name."

"Then why did you suggest we stay here? You said you should have warned me but you didn't. You knew what would happen, didn't you? You lied to me."

"Yes, Jack, I did. I knew what would happen," admitted Petucan. "But I'm not lying. You're still safe."

"So, if you love me, why would you do that to me? Why would you want me to have a nightmare?" accused Jack ignoring Petucan's last statement.

"Because you have to face your nightmares, Jack. You have to unpack them like you would open up a gift. You must take your nightmares out of the box you've stuffed them into so you can learn what are lies and what is the truth. I was helping you," explained Petucan.

"Helping me! Huh! Geez, thanks but no thanks! I didn't think you'd hurt me, Petucan. I trusted you."

"You can always trust me, Jack."

"How? You knew my nightmare would come back. You hurt me."

"Did I hurt you? Or are you just feeling hurt? They are two different things, Jack. When we lie to ourselves, the lies will surface so we can feel them.

Lies never lie low. It's the lie that hurts because it's hiding the truth."

"So, how do I know what's true?" asked Jack.

Petucan pointed. "Look into the pool of water, Jack. That's where the lies disappear. They can't live in the water because water is transparent. That is where truth is revealed."

Jack looked into the soft velvet eyes of Petucan. They shone with love. They smiled with trust. And they looked back at him with courage. He turned toward the pool of water, which was bright and clear even though it was dark this deep inside the cave. It was as if the pool had a light of its own. It glowed softly, caressing the walls with a warm blue light that rippled in a dance from an unknown song. As Jack leaned over the edge of the boulder, making sure he didn't lean too far so he wouldn't fall in, he looked for the truth. He looked and looked. Like an unknown song, the truth eluded him.

"I can't see anything," he said.

"That's just another lie," said Petucan. "Look again but don't look too hard. Sometimes, the truth is right in front of you."

Jack continued looking. All he saw was his reflection silhouetted by the pool's soft blue glow. He looked and looked as his reflection stared back.

"Perhaps you're still not ready to see the truth yet," advised Petucan. "Only by seeing the truth can you meet Satya in the quiet place. Satya is the dreamer of all dreams, and dreams are true for whoever is doing the dreaming."

Jack had been so distracted, he had almost forgotten about Satya. It was as if Satya was resting in the back of his mind, and now, Satya was being called forth from the pages of his memory.

"Perhaps your monkey-mind is still too noisy," said Petucan.

"The only noise I can hear is a chattering monkey in my head. You're the noisy one, not me," said Jack with a little frustration.

He sighed and went back to looking into the pool. The only thing that confronted him was his reflection. He tried to be very quiet as he looked. He almost didn't dare breathe as he looked back at himself. The two Jacks stared at each another. One stared down. One stared up. The harder they stared at each other, the more the images blurred. It was hard to tell who was staring at whom.

Jack was beginning to warm as his head began to spin. Faster and faster his head spun and he started to sweat. He closed his eyes as his pajamas began to stick to his body. Heat struck the top of his head as the earth shifted beneath him. When he opened his eyes, he was kneeling in sand. The daylight was blinding, the desert barren. There were sand dunes in every direction. He stood up quickly and touched Petucan and Ivanhoe to make sure they were still real. They were real all right, in a stuffed animal sort of way, and this was a real desert, in a dream sort of way.

✌✌ CHAPTER 11 ✌✌

STUCKERPILLERS

"We're in a desert," observed Jack aloud, getting used to bouncing from one place to another.

It was not much different from his real life because he was used to being bounced around. Real life or a dream, it didn't seem to matter anymore. He wasn't sure if he even cared. He got up and immediately noticed the dry air as the sun scorched the earth. He began to walk, uncertain if he was going backwards or forwards.

As they walked across the sandy dunes with no particular destination in mind, Jack began to tire. The sand sucked at his slippers as the sun sucked the moisture from his body. Petucan and Ivanhoe didn't seem affected at all by the blistering heat. They were lucky because they didn't sweat. Being stuffed with cotton had its advantages after all, Jack silently noted as the sun began to push their shadows ahead. He squinted his eyes at the shimmer in the distance. He thought the heat was waving at him until he recognized the tall palms.

"Look," he pointed, "Palm trees."

"It's an oasis. We can get some water and rest for a while," said Petucan.

As with most things seen from afar, it seemed to take forever to get there, just like a story takes a long time to find a reader.

Their shadows appeared to mock them as they raced ahead with the lowering of the sun at their backs. The sand found a new home between Jack's toes and began to scratch, trying to get under his skin. His damp pajamas chafed him under his arms and between his legs. He felt raw and adrift in a hostile environment. It was not much different from the children's home, he thought. He was a condition of nature forever moving and changing.

Just like the sand beneath his feet, the arid desert moved with the whims of the wind and the mind of the observer. Even the sky transformed into a deep solitary blue as Jack's shadow stretched ahead pulling at him, transforming him, making him part of the desert. Hot, thirsty and sleepy, he followed the dunes as they marched towards the oasis nestling on the horizon.

Jack wore down to a mindless physical body. Only his feet worked as if they understood where they must tread. He was lost in his need to rest and restore with only palm trees to beckon him forward. He heeded the call and soon the oasis appeared closer on the screen of his eyes. The picture was welcoming as the spring moved towards him with a promise to quench his thirst. Nothing else existed. Lack of water, lack of food, lack of nurture, lack of family—it was all the same. It's what Jack lacked in this moment but his longing was in reach. He could see it. He could taste it. Water—the elixir of life. His life depended on it. Just a few more steps.

Upon reaching the oasis, the first thing Jack did was cup his hands in the spring and gulp. He then splashed water over his head to cool. As soon as his immediate need was met, he sat underneath the nearest palm tree and snatched off his slippers. The offending sand found itself rudely evicted.

As Jack looked around, he saw the large spring gleaming back at him. Once again it pulled at his throat. Now, he could savor it. His mind came back with his taste buds. The water was delicious. It was a strange thought knowing that water had no taste yet tasted so good. As Jack cupped the water between his hands, he looked to each side of him and was surprised to see Petucan and Ivanhoe drinking too.

"Um, won't you get all soggy?" he asked even though he had seen them drink on the Mindless Express.

In his deep voice, Ivanhoe answered first, "Water is wet and soggy we get. But we won't sink because of a drink."

"If we dry out too much, we'll get brittle and break," continued Petucan. "But a little water won't hurt us. In fact, we even need to be washed from time to time."

Jack looked at Ivanhoe. He'd had Ivanhoe for many years and in all this time, he had never thought of giving him a bath. Now he looked closely and saw how dirty and matted he was. He was beginning to feel guilty at having neglected his best friend. The guilt got heavier when he saw the space where an eye should have been and a half-ripped ear. He stopped his drinking, sat down and put his arms around Ivanhoe. He gave him a long apologetic squeeze. It was a squeeze of regret and a hope for forgiveness.

It was then he realized he'd been so wrapped up in his own misery that he had caused more misery for Ivanhoe. Perhaps that's exactly what had happened to his parents. Perhaps they were so miserable together, they ended up causing him misery in turn. They probably didn't do it on purpose. They just didn't think. They were too wrapped up in themselves. The sadness enveloped Jack like a heavy blanket. Did his parents have any regrets? Did they really know what they were doing when they had made him and then walked away, leaving him alone? Could he forgive them?

Jack had not purposely neglected Ivanhoe. He hadn't realized what he was doing when he got angry and threw him on the floor. He hadn't taken much notice when Ivanhoe had lost an eye and ripped his ear. Now he saw.

Ivanhoe intuitively sang in his deep voice, "Your mom and dad were just as sad. They couldn't see and caused misery. They named you Jack and didn't look back. They got lost and you were the cost."

"Ivanhoe is right. That's what it cost them, Jack," said Petucan. "They'll never know what you will become. They will miss your best years and the potential you have within you. They closed themselves off when they left you. You shouldn't do the same. Don't close yourself off. It's not your fault. You're not to blame, Jack. Forgive yourself for thinking so and forgive yourself for Ivanhoe."

Jack hugged Ivanhoe even tighter as Petucan continued, "It's only when you are able to forgive that you can begin to move forward. You still have your future and so much opportunity ahead of you."

Jack gulped down more regret and with tears in his eyes, he said, "I cost Ivanhoe his eye and a ripped ear. I'm just as bad. Look at his fur. It's dirty and lumpy. I'm just like my mom and dad. I hurt him. I hurt Ivanhoe," he wept.

With a smile, Ivanhoe sang in his deep voice, "You did what you did 'cause your feelings were hid. There's only now, the time to forgive. There's nothing to fear for now you see clear. Your friendship, your love, in my heart I hold dear."

"Oh Ivanhoe. I love you so much. I'm sorry, Ivanhoe. I'm sorry I hurt you."

Petucan put his small hand on Jack's shoulder as if shouldering a great responsibility.

"Ivanhoe will always love you, Jack. But you have to love yourself. You have to forgive yourself. Everyone does something that needs forgiveness. It's impossible to live a life where you don't have to say you're sorry. But the most important person to say sorry to is yourself. If you can forgive yourself for your actions, you'll be able to forgive your mom and dad for their actions."

Jack jumped and a shiver ran up his spine. It was not Petucan's words that had shook him. Jack was shaken by a strange furry thing that had dropped out of the palm tree and landed right by his side with a soft thud. It was a fat ball of fur that quickly stretched out to nearly eight inches long.

Forgetting his tears, Jack immediately jumped to his feet and scrabbled back only to fall down on his butt as the sand slid beneath him. He felt his heart begin to thump as the snow-white fur began wobbling towards him. It didn't seem dangerous but it was like nothing he'd seen before. Jack was about to stand and take another step back when the snow-white fur began to wobble away in the opposite direction. Jack quickly got over his fright as curiosity kicked in. He knelt in the sand to take a closer look but fell back on his butt as it wobbled towards him again.

"Don't worry, Jack, it won't hurt you," said Petucan.

"Riiight, I've heard that one before," responded Jack thinking of the mountain lyings.

Petucan walked over to the snow-white fur and picked it up, stroking it with his other hand. The snow-white fur let out a musical trill and began to stretch out at least another six inches.

"They love to sing when they're stroked," said Petucan seeing Jack's astonished look.

Jack stood up and standing by Petucan, put his hand in the deep fur until it disappeared.

"It's so soft," observed Jack out loud as he also began to stroke it, listening to the tuneful trilling. "What is it?"

"It's a stuckerpiller," answered Petucan.

"A stuck-a-what?"

"A stuckerpiller," Petucan repeated.

"What the heck's a stuckerpiller?"

"Look up," directed Petucan.

As Jack looked up, he could see that the leaves of the palm tree were covered in snow-white fur.

"Wow. There's lots of them. What are they?" he asked again.

Gently, Petucan rolled it over and Jack could see eight small hands sticking out from the white fur, or were they feet? He couldn't quite tell. But what surprised him the most were the beautiful green eyes, pink nose and small pink lips smiling up at him. Surprised, because they were at both ends. There were two faces.

"Whoa," said Jack confused.

Petucan smiled. He enjoyed surprises especially when someone else was getting the surprise. He also liked sharing what he knew.

"I know. Cute, isn't it?" said Petucan.

"It's different. Yeah, I guess it's cute in a funny sorta way. How come it's got two heads?" asked Jack.

"Because it's a stuckerpiller," answered Petucan. "When they are born, they only have one head. But when they meet another stuckerpiller they really like, they become inseparable. They eventually end up stuck together. They can't come apart anymore, and they have to rely on each other for everything. They become entirely co-dependent."

"Oh, I see," said Jack not seeing at all. "So... um," he started with embarrassment at his next question, "There's no back end, so... um... how do they poop?"

"They barf," Petucan laughed.

And no sooner had Petucan explained when a loud pop resulted in a green slimy fur ball splatting right in the center of Jack's pajama pocket.

"Yuk. That's gross," cried Jack quickly stepping out of the way when the other end opened its mouth.

With a resounding pop, the second fur ball landed right on the tip of Ivanhoe's nose. Ivanhoe immediately shook his head flicking the slime in all directions, not at all pleased with being used as a toilet. After washing off the green slimy fur ball in the spring, both Jack and Ivanhoe made sure they kept out of firing range.

"I'm glad I'm not a stuckerpiller," said Jack. "They're yucky. I'd hate to have to barf all the time. That's just so gross."

"You're not that much different," said Petucan as he resumed his stroking, encouraging the stuckerpiller to continue trilling musically.

"What do you mean? I don't look anything like it," claimed Jack.

"It's got nothing to do with looks," answered Petucan.

"Then what're you talking about?"

Petucan went on to explain, "They are called stuckerpillers because they get stuck together. They depend so much on each other even when they become unhappy living together. They can't leave each other because they've become one. They lose their own identity and then they get confused. They become helpless. When one stuckerpiller wants to go in one direction and the other stuckerpiller wants to go in the opposite direction, they end up pulling against each other, never really getting anywhere."

"So, I am different," stated Jack. "I don't have two faces and I don't go around barfing. And, no one's pulling me away from where I want to go," he added for good measure.

"Are you sure, Jack? I know you feel sick inside when you're really upset and then you barf out angry words even when you're the only one that hears them. You know you do, Jack. And you don't need two faces to be stuck. One face will do. When you're truly stuck, it's difficult to choose which direction to go in. You end up in limbo. You get stuck in a rut," explained Petucan.

Not wanting to be left out, Ivanhoe sang in his deep voice, "You're stuck in the head so you can't get ahead.

You only look back so a future you lack. You're stuck on your mom and don't have fun. You're stuck on your dad and only get sad."

For Jack, that was a very sad song indeed. But, deep down, Jack knew the truth when heard it. It was true. He was stuck. Stuck in the memories of a mom and dad he couldn't remember. Just like quicksand, his past always pulling at him, holding him back.

Looking at the stuckerpiller, Jack was stuck in a pillar of sadness. Attached and dependent on parents that no longer existed for him. His memories sucked at him, drawing him in like a dream.

Sensing Jack's thoughts, Petucan put the stuckerpiller down by the trunk of the palm tree. Jack could see the stuckerpiller trying to climb the tree while the other end, which was trying to go in the other direction, held it back.

"It will probably take them two days to climb up that tree unless the other end is stronger," said Petucan.

"But what if the other end is stronger?" asked an unhappy Jack.

"It will probably end up in the water and dissolve," answered Petucan.

That made Jack even more miserable.

"That's how life works, Jack. When you get too attached and can't let go, you'll become a slave to whatever you're holding on to. You'll dissolve without growing into your full potential. You'll stay stuck in a past that no longer exists. You don't have to be stuck, Jack. You don't have to allow your memories to drag you away from your future," encouraged Petucan.

"I can't forget, even though I've forgotten what they looked like. I can't just make my memories disappear. It's there in my head. It makes me sad. Then I get angry and end up crying because it hurts. I had a mom and dad who left me," said an unsmiling Jack.

"Yes, you did. But you don't have to forget them or cling to the idea that they threw you away. It's just an idea, Jack. You cannot know their true reasons. You can only know how you feel. You can feel angry and sad, happy or mad. Your feelings can teach you a lot. But you're more than your feelings, Jack. You can be anything you want to be. You only need to trust yourself. You're not a throwaway. You can depend on yourself. Trust yourself, Jack," urged Petucan.

"I'm tired," Jack sighed as he turned his back on Petucan. He watched the last of the sun's rays stretch on the horizon before they sank below the surface of Dhyāna Land.

It was cooler once the sun decided to leave, so they huddled together and soon fell into a deep desert sleep. The quietness covered Jack's sadness as the sand sighed and settled beneath their bodies.

"Wake up! Come on, Jack, wake up!" nudged the soft voice.

Jack lifted his strawberry blond hair out of his eyes and blinked at the gentle sun. It was morning. He had slept so soundly, there was not a shade of bad dream to touch the new day. He felt whole, full of life and empty of food.

"Here you go," said Petucan putting a handful of figs in his lap as Ivanhoe dropped a coconut from his mouth. Bashing two coconuts together, they managed to crack one open.

They fed on figs and coconut washed down with coconut milk. As they got up to leave, Jack turned to see the stuckerpiller stuck halfway up the palm tree. "Well, at least it won't dissolve in the water," he thought as he turned away.

They left the oasis and headed towards a new day and a new experience. That's what Jack knew deep inside of him. He knew only he could experience each moment and right now, he began to experience something new. Something he hadn't noticed before.

He felt your eyes reading these words on this page, trying to fathom out his story. He knew deep down that only he could live his story, not you. Your eyes looking into his dream have their own story. Your story that only you can truly experience because it's seen with your eyes and told with your voice. Jack hasn't heard your story, but he was beginning to hear loud and clear.

It started with an unforgiving whistle in his inner ear that got louder and louder the more he listened. He tried to hear the sounds of silence and only heard noise. It was as if the quiet desert was coming alive and getting closer to his one recurring nightmare.

෪ড় CHAPTER 12 ෪ড়

ETHOS THE GIANT OGRE

Jack tried to shake the sounds from his head to regain the quiet but there was no quiet to be heard. He tried to concentrate and silence the noise from bubbling up. The harder Jack concentrated on being quiet, the more noise he could hear. He heard his eardrums begin to boom. He heard birds crying in the air. Even the wind urgently whispered in his ears. Soon, his head was a confusion of noise. He closed his eyes to try and block out the sounds.

Sounds of thunder exploded around him. The wind howled with pain. He could feel cold hard rain beating upon his soft strawberry blond head. He could feel his heart beating even harder in his chest.

For Jack, this was a nightmare indeed. He knew they were no longer in the desert. As he opened his eyes, he could see the dark rocks looming before him. Feel them gathering, closing in. Above him were thick branches jutting out from the rocks. The branches reached toward him, slapping him across his face. The stones beneath his feet began to shift and crumble as if the black earth wanted to open wide and swallow him up. The sky was dark. Not a single star could be seen. Only the moon gave light as it struggled between the roiling thunder clouds. Ivanhoe barked out loud when he heard Petucan screech and saw him running toward Jack's side.

"Petucan, it's okay. It's only a bad dream. It's really safe. Isn't that what you always tell me when I have a bad dream?" asked a trembling Jack trying to be brave.

"Yes. But I also told you that dreams are real dreams," said Petucan squeezing tightly onto Jack's hand.

The icy cold rain stung their faces as the thunder clapped in fury across the vicious sky. Lightning streaked angrily, chasing them deeper into the dark forest. As the lightning flashed, Jack's eyes opened wide. He saw something huge and terrible. A giant black shadow with glowing red eyes stared back at him. Jack knew he had seen the ominous creature before.

Evil and threatening, the creature trundled towards him. Jack was again dreaming his bad dream. Now he remembered. He was once again face-to-face with his enemy, Ethos the Giant Ogre. The boy-eating monster would chase Jack across Dhyāna Land, right into the land of wakefulness. Then Ethos would slide into the depths of his mind until next time. Always, Petucan would wake him out of his bad dream, but now, he had to save Petucan and Ivanhoe. He had to face Ethos the Giant Ogre once and for all.

"Stay there, you'll be safe," shouted Jack above the roar of thunder as he pushed Petucan and Ivanhoe behind a large tree.

"Safe! Ha! Ha! Ha!" boomed the hideous voice. "Nothing is safe from me. When I have finished with you, I will have your friends for dessert."

Jack spun on his heels as the giant ogre swept sharp claws through the air. He ran as fast as he could in and out of the trees. Ethos the Giant Ogre hissed and spat as its huge bulk smashed the trees into the ground. Nothing could stand in its way. Terrified, Jack ran faster into the forest. He felt trapped. There seemed nowhere for him to run and hide.

"Ethos, you're a giant ogre. You're a monster. Leave us alone," shouted Jack in his scared but commanding voice.

"I know what I am, but please, you can call me EGO for short," mocked the giant ogre. "Ha! Ha! Ha! Now you're mine."

"NO!" screamed Jack. "I won't let you get me or my friends."

"You have no choice, little boy. I am the darkness of your dreams. You cannot wake up this time," boomed the voice above the thunder.

As lightning flashed across the sky, the giant ogre moved closer. With furious eyes of dancing fire, the giant ogre grinned. Razor-sharp teeth glinted in the shadowy moonlight. Jack whirled around and fell backwards. The nightmare was right in front of him. Just another step and he would fall into the clutches of Ethos the Giant Ogre.

"So, little boy, do you really think you can escape me? Huh! I am always lurking in the darkness. There is no escape. You can run to the end of your dreams but you can't hide from me."

"I'm not afraid to face you. It doesn't matter how big you are. You are in my dream and I can dream what I like," shouted Jack, remembering Petucan's words.

"Then you had better dream quickly because I like strawberry blond hair and freckles. I wonder if you taste like strawberries. I'll soon find out," bellowed the giant ogre.

Jack knew what he must do. He must dream that the storm was his to command. He stood his ground and silenced his thoughts. He became still as a statue and began to dream. He concentrated on merging with the storm. He became one with the energy that surrounded him. It only took a moment; and he was in that moment, as if time no longer existed.

He dreamt the storm becoming fiercer. The storm obeyed. With an army of gales, the tempest became stronger. Even the storm knew what it must do. Unleashing its weapons, the storm channeled the white heat. A flash of lightning emerged with a scowl. It coursed through the dark sky heading towards them. Thunder echoed in Jack's ears. The ground shook as a bright white bolt came crashing to the earth. The trees split around them.

Jack was quicker. Because it was his dream, he knew what was coming next. He jumped out from under a falling branch. He slipped towards the giant ogre and spotted a gap between the ogre's legs. He ran through the gap and fell again just as a huge branch came crashing down, right on top the ogre's head.

His enemy and worst nightmare sailed past him smacking hard to the ground. The ground shuddered as the huge bulk dented the earth beneath the heavy limb. Down and out went the ominous bulk, down into the depths of darkness, the depths of unconsciousness.

Jack scrambled to his feet as Petucan and Ivanhoe came running towards him. They all looked as the giant ogre melted into the earth never to be seen again.

❧❧ CHAPTER 13 ❧❧

TIME FOR QUIET

The storm breathed a sigh of relief as quietness began to bloom.

"Jack, you're so brave. You faced Ethos the Giant Ogre. Oh Jack, I was so afraid," said Petucan trembling softly. "I knew you had nightmares, but I didn't realize they were that bad. You were brave and you faced your fear."

"Petucan, it was you I listened to. You were the voice in my head that helped me. You taught me to believe

I could make anything happen. I can travel anywhere I want. I can choose what to dream. I dreamt that the storm was my friend and it helped me. I dreamt I was the storm," said Jack shivering from his encounter with Ethos the Giant Ogre.

"You were very brave. Thank you for saving us," said Petucan emerging out of his fright.

It was Ivanhoe's turn to thank his master for saving them so in his deep voice he sang, "It's not too soon that it's over for Ethos the Giant Ogre. Jack's courage was mightier. Our future looks brighter."

"Ivanhoe is right, Jack. Your future is brighter. Now you know you can weather any storm life throws at you."

"I can," said Jack. "You're right. I CAN!"

"You bet you can!" said Petucan.

The night gave way as the day began to lighten. The sun peeked through the thunder clouds and then suddenly burst forth, shedding the grey weight of the storm. The trees sighed in relief as the howling wind left their branches. Flowers came out from their hiding places, bowing low to Jack in thanks for making the day beautiful. Even the tall grass shivered and clapped in applause with what had just passed and being blessed with another wonderful day.

Jack sat down upon a large boulder. He looked at his ever-faithful friend Ivanhoe. He looked at Petucan, at how he shone with love.

He felt so weary right now. He was tired from the fight he had fought—the same fight he had fought each time he slept. The same fight he had fought when he was awake. But now he knew. He knew he would not have to fight his worst enemy ever again. He knew because he now had the secret to his bad dreams.

Jack forgave his dreams. He forgave himself for dreaming them. He felt his heart lift as he forgave parents that didn't know how to be his mom and dad. He felt release from his past because now he finally understood that he could dream whatever he liked. He now knew he has the choice to make his dreams good or bad, even during the daytime. He didn't have to listen to the bullies that chased him. He didn't have to believe their lies. He didn't have to lie to himself anymore. He didn't have to lie because he knew he was worthy. He was worthy of love. This was the truth and the truth lived in him. Jack now knew. He now believed.

Truth is beautiful. All Jack had to do was imagine a sunny day, and if he looked towards the sun, the shadows would fall behind. When a storm came by, if he concentrated hard enough, he could listen to the music of the falling rain and perhaps look for rainbows.

"This is such a perfect dream, Petucan. I can dream what I like. I will always look for the bright things in my dreams. The bright things are everything I love. I love you and Ivanhoe. You're my very best friends."

"We love you too, Jack, and you're right, you can dream what you like, even when you're awake, which is the best dream of all. There isn't anyone who can dream your dreams for you. It's up to you, just like it's up to everyone else to dream their own dreams."

Ivanhoe sung in his deep voice, "We have all seen it's a perfect dream. You make your choice because you have a voice."

As their hearts began to lighten and lift, Jack, Petucan and his ever-faithful friend Ivanhoe danced and sang together with so much happiness and laughter. The beautiful day was a song to be sung, a dance to be danced.

"Petucan, I almost forgot what I was searching for: Satya, the dreamer of all dreams. I don't believe I need Satya's help anymore, but I would like to meet Satya. Which way do I turn to find the quiet place?" Jack asked looking around.

"You have already been there," answered Petucan with a smile.

Jack smiled too. Yes. He had already been there but had never realized it until now. It was a quiet bright place that resided in the stillness between dreams and reality. It was a place made so bright with all the love that lived inside of him. The same love we all have shining inside of us. Jack now understood for the very first time. He now understood that each and every one of us is a light of peace. A light of love. A light of truth. We can choose to shine our light with everyone we meet. We can choose because we have a voice.

Jack's voice in his head became very quiet.

The time was *now*. No other time existed.

Now was the time for quiet.

So, Jack, Petucan and Ivanhoe became very still and very quiet.

Very quiet were the trees, flowers and grass. Even the rocks stood still and silent. The wind sighed as it left the afternoon sky towing the clouds away. The sun gently shone down upon the quietness.

So very quiet.

So quiet.

Only the silence could be heard above the quiet.

141

The silence, like a door opening, gave way to the pure white light gently pulsating with so much love.

Jack felt the love inside him and all around him. A peaceful joy filled his heart. The light of love was everywhere. In Petucan. In Ivanhoe. In the trees and the rocks. In the sunshine and flowers.

Satya, the dreamer of all dreams, guided Jack back to the waterfall; the waterfall of life—a life of rainbows, ripples and splashes.

Jack smiled. He smiled because he knew he was Satya. There was no difference. He was truth. He was love. He was Satya, the beloved. He was the dreamer of all his dreams.

"Hey, wake up! Come on, Jack, wake up!" said the gentle voice.

The small, strawberry blond head looked up from the pillow. The soft blue eyes focused upon the figure standing over him.

"It's me, Jack. Come on, wake up!" said his Auntie Joyce as she gently stroked his hair. "You've got a big day today."

As Jack sat up in bed, he saw the soft golden glow of his Auntie Joyce's silhouette as the sun eased through the gap in the curtains. He widened his eyes and smiled. He hadn't realized how cuddly she was.

He hadn't realized how her eyes sparkled and danced when she smiled. Now he saw. He saw her love.

"Auntie Joyce, I had a dream about Petucan. He's a monkey, and my dog Ivanhoe was there. I met Patrick the leprechaun and had to fight Ethos the Giant Ogre. I dreamt of Satya filled with lots of love and a waterfall and bright lights and rainbows. It was the best dream I've ever had," said Jack in a rush.

His Auntie Joyce had never heard Jack speak so much. He was usually so very quiet. She beamed inside when she saw his smile.

As she listened patiently, Jack continued with his colorful story of a cheeky genie, mountain lyings and stuckerpillers. He told of meeting AlberJohn Berry and Lady Felicity. He related his journey on the Mindless Express and laughed about the boy on the rock with a bright red sock.

His Auntie Joyce made sure she didn't interrupt him. She had never realized before how imaginative Jack could be. "He's going to be a storyteller one day," she said to herself, loving his happy adventure.

Ivanhoe smiled and silently sang in his deep voice, "From the waterfall, we understand all. There is nothing above a world full of love."

And that's where you'll find Satya, in a world full of love. Satya is *truth* and the truth lives in all things seen and unseen.

Another beautiful day. Another wonderful dream.

But the dream didn't end there.

❧❧ CHAPTER 14 ❧❧

HAPPY JACK

"That's a lovely story, Jack. Now come on, young man; up and out of bed. You've got a big day today. Don't you remember?" smiled Auntie Joyce.

Jack did remember. After school, he was going to meet a family who were looking to adopt a boy. They were coming to see if he wanted to spend some time with them. They wanted to get to know the little boy they had heard so much about from the welfare office. And, it was an opportunity for him to get to know them. He was told they had already adopted a little girl who was a year younger than Jack.

Jack wasn't sure what to think about this. In fact, it was pretty hard to think about anything right now because his nightmare had turned into the best dream he had ever had. And his best dream was lying with truth deep down inside of him.

He knew it was true. He knew love existed even if he couldn't feel it all the time. He knew he was brave even though he had run away from bullies. He knew happiness existed because he had felt it in his heart. He felt it inside of him now. And best of all, he knew his dream didn't have to end. He could dream whatever he liked, even when he was awake. He could dream he didn't have to run away. He knew how to dream.

"Dreams are real dreams," he said to himself.

As Jack walked to school that day, he thought about his adventures with Ivanhoe and Petucan. The more he thought of the colorful monkey, the more he could hear his chatter. Petucan's chattering got louder... and louder... and louder. Jack's mind was a-chatter.

"Happy Jack, Happy Jack, run far away. Happy Jack, Happy Jack, don't you come back," came the sounds from behind.

As Jack turned, he saw that the bullies were on his trail. He watched them approach menacingly, nudging one another.

Jack's stomach was in his heart and his heart was in his throat. He took a big gulp and swallowed his fear. He decided the time for running was over. Instead, he turned and faced them full on waving a friendly hand in the air and then began walking towards them, noticing their confusion as they slowed. There were five of them. As Jack neared the group, they stopped right in front of him, uncertain of what they were going to experience. Alarmed, because Jack had always run away when they had chased him. This was something new. This was unpredictable.

Jack lowered his hand and greeted the nearest boy. "Hello Caleb, hello Tom," he said as he turned towards Tom. "Hello Cassie, hello Mark, hello Damon," he said as he looked them in the eye. And then he smiled as he heard them mutter an awkward hello under their breath. He smiled his best smile ever.

"Can I walk to school with you?" Jack asked.

The would-be bullies never moved from the spot. They stood speechless, looking at one another as they tried to understand what was happening. Instead of waiting for an answer, Jack turned toward the school, steady in his courage and lighter in his footsteps.

"Er, sure," answered Tom waking from his momentary shock.

Jack continued on his way wondering if the element of surprise would wear off and the bullies would begin chasing him again. They didn't chase him. They followed him at a short distance.

He made it all the way to school without incident. However, the element of surprise had not worn off for Jack. The surprise stayed with him throughout the whole day. He was surprised by his own actions, and he was even more surprised by the bullies' reactions because they hadn't reacted at all. He had put them at a loss and stopped them in their tracks.

He was beginning to understand the value of facing his fears. He realized his power was in how he acted regardless of the outcome. He knew they couldn't do anything worse to him that he hadn't already experienced. If they had pushed him around, at least he knew he would have tried instead of just running away. But that hadn't happened. They had left him alone. And because they had left him alone, he knew he would never, ever be alone again. He had found himself. He could rely on himself. He could be all he could be and then some.

Throughout the day, Jack thought about the family he was going to meet. He wondered if they'd like him. He wondered if he'd like them. You can't like or dislike what you don't know, he concluded.

As he walked home from school, he thought about the future. He thought about the immediate future because he was hungry. He hoped they were having Chinese this evening. He loved Chinese food, especially the little Chinese dumplings. However, as he neared the children's home, his light heart began to dim some.

His feet began to feel heavier and his pace began to slow. His big day was upon him. He wasn't sure what to expect but was nervous all the same. As he climbed the steps one at a time and opened the big door, he stepped into a quiet hallway. He wasn't sure why, but it seemed very, very quiet. As he walked further down the hall, he began to hear chattering in the small room to the left, which served as an office for the children's home.

"Okay, Mrs. Hankins, I'll let him know. Okay, thank you, I'll see you shortly. Bye."

Auntie Joyce came out of her office. "Oh, hello Jack, there you are. Mr. and Mrs. Hankins will be here in fifteen minutes. Why don't you go and wash up?" she suggested.

Jack went to the other end of the house, out of sight of Auntie Joyce. Instead of going upstairs to wash, he opened the back door and walked outside. In the garden, he pulled back the branches of the weeping willow tree and sat down. He was completely hidden from view. He put his books down by his side and sat, knees bent, elbows on knees and head cupped in his hands. He sat and his mind was quiet.

His thoughts escaped him. It was very quiet behind the long branches. Very quiet in a sleepy green sort of way. The quietness was complete. In the silence, Jack looked up and noticed all the different colors that surrounded him. Green leaves in sunshine and green leaves in shadow. Green grass creating intricate patterns of light as it bent this way and that.

"Thoughts are like that," Jack mused. "Thoughts come in all different shapes and shades. Some thoughts are sad and dark, and some thoughts are happy and light."

His mind continued to wander as he sat in the silence. He let his thoughts flow in and out without giving them much attention. It was like observing a dream winding down until his mind began to still. It was so quiet sitting there—so calm and so very quiet. Jack was at peace.

The quiet was disturbed by a rustle as the low branches parted each side like the curtains on a stage drawing back. He felt he was sitting in the front row waiting for a play to start.

The character on stage bowed and entered. The first thing he noticed was the light shining in the velvet brown eyes followed by honey-gold wavy hair and olive skin. As if on cue, the girl standing in from of him said, "Hello."

Jack looked at her and said nothing. He saw she wore a yellow dress, rainbow-patterned socks that rested in soft canvas shoes, and a matching rainbow-colored head band. As he looked, Jack was drawn to the stuffed toy dangling in her hand.

The young girl held a small monkey with a button nose and long tail. The monkey seemed to smile at him. It was a purple smile.

Jack smiled back and the little girl also smiled as she noticed Jack looking at her monkey.

"Her name is Samadhi. You can pet her if you like," the girl said as she held the small monkey towards him. "My name is Bryony. You're going to be my new brother. I've always wanted a brother," she continued.

Jack held out his hand and took the monkey. "Do you want to meet Ivanhoe?" he asked from the script he was writing in his mind. "He's my dog. He's not a real dog but he can be. He likes to be cuddled. By the way, my name's Jack. You can call me Happy Jack if you like," he continued smiling.

"You must be very happy if that's your name," Bryony said as they both walked into the house together, into a new family, into another dream.

"I am happy, Bryony. I like your name. Are you happy?" he asked.

"I AM," came the answer as a dream unfolded into reality.

❧ End ❧

About the Author

Born in London, England, Jacqueline acquired a love for travel and followed the sun to finally settle in sunny Florida where she lives with her husband and sixteen-year-old puppy dog. Her near-daughter, grandchildren and great granddaughter play nearby.

After spending over forty years in the corporate world, she purchased a magic mat, donned tight pants and stepped into her next adventure where…

"Ish bish, bish bosh, skiddle-dee-dee and skiddle-dee-do, make your wish now for it to come true."

"Geez! What the? Genie, what are you doing here? You made me jump."

"I'm here to grant you a wish."

"Can't you see I'm writing my bio? I don't need a wish. Please don't interrupt me."

"You don't need a wish, but you do wish for something."

"Everyone wishes for something or another. Now, if you don't mind, I'd like to finish writing my bio. Please go away."

"I can help you with your wish."

"Look, can't you see I'm busy?"

"You wish that wherever your mom went, she discovered peace and found a full and happy life."

"Genie please…"

"And you wish your dad continues to love and be loved."

"Okay genie, I do wish for those things, but as you know, you can make all the wishes you want. It won't make an iota of difference because everyone writes their own story. Now please let me finish."

"Ish bish, bish bo…"

"GENIE!!!"

"Okay, okay. Skiddle-dee-dee. Too-da-loo."

…as a yoga instructor, she inspires students to live their purpose in the present moment. The teachings of yoga presented the perfect moment for Jacqueline to share her life's journey.

Happy Jack is her debut novel and portrays the challenges of abandonment and growing up in a children's home.

Styled as a children's book, this philosophical story observes human nature and connectedness amid familiar struggles felt in today's world. Experienced first-hand by the author, this inspiring adult allegory is a search for courage, acceptance, forgiveness and inner peace.

Acknowledgements

I want to thank my mom and dad for the dawn of my journey. Without them, I would not be able to share my story.

Thank you to my family: Teresa, Louise (who is playing in Dream Land), Melanie, Raymond and Maisie. Thank you to my foster mom and dad, foster sister Bridie, and all my extended family. In your own way, you have shaped my life and fostered my spirit.

Thank you to my husband Wayne, near-daughter Amanda, granddaughters Ceionna and Kearra, and great granddaughter Kyla Raine for surrounding me with your love.

In memory of my dear friend Robin who gracefully fought her own heroic battle.

To my yoga community: Sunder for encouraging me to start a blog. I haven't stopped writing since. To Jaye and Rita for enriching my awareness and natural curiosity. To Shannon and Tracie for granting *Happy Jack* some of their valuable time. To all the yogis who invite me to guide their practice and put up with my 'Jackie Chats.' You know who you are.

To the monkey puzzle tree that stood guard outside my bedroom window.

And to you dear reader, who unsuspectingly grace page 130. Maybe one day it will be your story living in the minds and hearts of others.

Made in United States
Orlando, FL
10 April 2023

31956396R00095